A LOST W
WILDS OF THE ARCTIC

Only in dim legends did mankind remember Atlantis and the Lost Tribes, that is, until Victor Nelson's extraordinary adventure into the Arctic unknown. Nelson and his pal, Richard Alden, had been forced down during a flight over a previously unexplored Arctic region. Their situation was desperate. And when Alden became lost, Nelson knew it was only a matter of time before his pal would perish in the Arctic cold. But when he found traces of a bloody struggle, Nelson knew Alden had been taken—forcibly. But by who…and why? Soon Nelson found himself following a trail into a forgotten world—a world filled with prehistoric beasts and lost Atlantean civilizations. And it was in this fantastic realm that Victor Nelson soon found the adventure of a lifetime.

F. Van Wyck Mason's "Phalanxes of Atlans" is a true classic of early science fiction adventure.

AUTHOR PORTRAIT

F. Van Wyck Mason (1901-1978)

Table of Contents

PHALANXES OF ATLANS

By
F. VAN WYCK MASON

ARMCHAIR FICTION
PO Box 4369, Medford, Oregon 97504

CHAPTER ONE

THE ice suddenly gave way under his foot, hurling Victor Nelson violently forward to lie in the deep snow at the bottom of a tiny crevasse, down which the merciless gale moaned like an anguished demon.

"It's no use," he muttered bitterly. "We've fought hard, but we're done for."

He lay still, stupidly watching his breath form tiny beads of ice on the ends of the fur which lined his parka. Until that moment he had not realized how thoroughly exhausted he was. Every muscle of his starved, bruised body ached unbearably. It wasn't so bad lying there in the soft snow. He could rest, then look later for the ice hummock behind which the plane lay sheltered. Rest! That's what he needed, a good long rest.

But deep within him, a primal instinct stabbed his waning consciousness. "No," he gasped, and blinked his reddened eyes behind smoked goggles which dulled the shimmer of the aurora. "If I stop, I'll never get up."

Shaken by the terrific velocity of the arctic gale he numbly clambered to his feet, then stooped with a stiff awkward motion to retrieve a Winchester rifle which lay half buried in the snow beside the blurred imprint of his body.

"Wonder if Alden had any better luck?" The question burned dully in his brain. "Don't suppose so; there can't be anything alive in this God-awful wilderness." As he

Agile as grasshoppers, those fierce war dogs ripped and worried their prey...

PHALANXES OF ATLANS
By F. V. W. Mason

stumbled on he found no answer in an unbroken vista of wind-scored ice and drifting snow that, swirling high into the air, momentarily cut off the view of that black line of ice-capped mountains barely visible on the horizon.

"Yes, if he hasn't found anything, we'll be dead or frozen stiff before to-morrow."

His soul—that of a true explorer—revolted, not at the thought of death, but that his and Alden's courageously won discovery of a majestic mountain range towering high over a polar region marked "unexplored" on the maps would now never be made public.

Leaning forward against the merciless icy blast he painfully picked his way over a treacherous ice ridge, to be faintly encouraged by the fact that the towerlike hummock of ice marking the position of the plane now lay but a few hundred yards ahead.

Bitterly he cursed that demon of ill-fortune who had sent the blinding snow storm which had forced down the plane ten long days ago at the very beginning of its triumphant return flight to the base at Cape Richards. Since that hour the storm gods had emptied the vials of their wrath upon the luckless explorers. Day after day, cyclonic winds made all thought of a take-off suicidal in the extreme. Three days ago the last of their food had given out, and, he mused, starvation is an ill companion for despair.

Slip, slide and fall! On he fought until the final barrier was reached and he stood staring hopelessly down into a small natural amphitheater which sheltered the great monoplane. The ship was still there, its engine snugged in a canvas shroud and with the soft, dry snow banked up high in the lee of its silver gray fuselage. Numbly, like a man in the grip of a painful coma, Nelson shielded his face with a furry hand to scan the surrounding terrain. "Hell!" The door block of the igloo they had built was still snowed up; Alden was not there!

"He's not back," he muttered, while his body swayed beneath the gale which smote him with fierce, unseen fists. "Poor devil, I hope he hasn't lost the way."

All the bitterness of undeserved defeat stung his soul as he started down the incline into the hollow.

SUDDENLY he paused. The rifle flew into the ready position and his chilled thumb drew back the hammer. "What's this?" On the snow at his feet was a bright, scarlet splash, dreadfully distinct against the white background. While his dazed brain struggled to register what his eyes saw, he looked to the right and left and discovered several more of the hideous spots. Then an object that gleamed dully in the polar twilight attracted his attention. He lumbered forward, stooped stiffly and caught up a long, half round strip of bronze.

"What? Why? Oh—I'm crazy. I'm seeing things!" The pain in his empty stomach was now becoming excruciating. To steady himself he shut his eyes, shook his head as though to clear it, then looked again at that strip of metal in his hand. Attached to it were two slender strips of leather like straps, ending in small, bronze buckles.

"Why, it's not from the plane," he stammered aloud. "Damned if it doesn't look like a greave the old Greek warriors used to wear to protect their shins."

Suddenly alarmed and mystified beyond words, he shuffled forward over the snow, the greave yet clutched in a fur gloved hand. Presently two more objects, already half buried by the stinging, swirling drifts, caught his attention. One was the stock of Alden's rifle, protruding starkly brown from the unrelieved whiteness, and the other was a broken wooden shaft that ended a graceful but wickedly sharp bronze spear head.

"I've either gone crazy," he said, "or I'm delirious. Yes, I must be clean nutty! There *couldn't* be a human settlement within a thousand miles. Let's see what's happened."

ON the snow of a little wind-sheltered space behind the igloo he discovered the unmistakable and ominous signs of a struggle. An indefinite number of footprints, blurred but enormous in size, were marked in the snow. Here and there deep furrows mutely testified how Alden and the enemies against whom he struggled had reeled back and forth in vicious combat over a considerable area. Then, shaken by a new fear, he discovered Alden's left glove and a rag of some peculiar thick material that seemed to have a metallic finish. But what aroused his gravest fears were the numerous splashes of blood that here and there streaked the snow in gruesome relief.

Only a moment Nelson stood, shaken by the merciless wind, scanning the piece of bronzed armor between his gloved hands with a fresh interest. It was beautifully fashioned, and decorated at the knee point with the wonderfully wrought figure of a dolphin.

If he could only think clearly! But his brain seemed to lie in a red-hot skull. "Whatever's happened," he muttered, "I'd better not waste time; they couldn't have been here so long ago. Poor Alden! I wonder what kind of devils caught him?"

EVEN before he had finished the sentence the aviator had taken up the partially obliterated trail of spattered blood drops. That what he sought appeared to be a marauding party of giants restrained him not at all. The one clear thought burning in his weary brain was that Richard Alden, his best friend—the man with whom he had traveled over half the world, by whose side he had faced many a perilous situation—must at that moment lie in peril, the extent of which he could only surmise.

"Must have been about a dozen of them," he said thickly. And, holding the Winchester ready, he commenced once more to plod on through the stinging sheets of wind-driven ice particles. More than once he had great difficulty in not losing that crimson trail, for here and there the restless, white crystals completely blotted out the splashes.

All at once Nelson checked his pathetically slow progress, finding himself on the top of an eminence, looking down in what appeared to be a vastly deep natural amphitheater of snow and ice. At the bottom, and perhaps a hundred yards distant, was a curious black oval from which appeared to rise a dense, wind-whipped column of whitish vapor.

"My eyes must be going back on me," muttered Nelson through stiffened lips. How intolerably heavy his fur suit seemed! His strength was about gone and that curious black mouthlike circle seemed infinitely far away. But, spurred by fears for his friend, he started downward for the precipitious trail leading directly towards it.

Once he stepped inside the crater, he became conscious of a terrific side pressure which gripped him as a whirlpool seizes a luckless swimmer. The wind buffetted him from all angles, dealing him powerful blows on face and body, which, too strong for his weary body, sent him reeling weakly, drunkenly across the hard, glare ice towards the vortex. Twice he slipped, each time finding it harder to arise. But at last he approached what on closer inspection proved to be a subterranean vent of black rock.

"Steam!" he gasped. "It's steam coming out of there!"

SWAYED by a dozen conflicting emotions, he paused, the Winchester barrel wavering like a reed in his enfeebled grasp.

"The whole thing's crazy," he decided. "I must be frozen and lying somewhere, delirious. Poor Dick! Can't help him much now."

Like a man in a nightmare who advances but feels nothing under his feet, Nelson staggered on towards that huge, gaping aperture of black rock. On the threshold a pool of melted snow water made him stare.

"Hell!" he said. "It's only a volcanic vent of some kind." Then dimly came the recollection of Eskimo legends concerning thermal springs beyond the desolate and unknown reaches of Grant Land.

His mind in an indescribable turmoil, Nelson splashed across a hundred yards of sodden snow, then shivered on wading knee deep through a pool of melted ice. Now he stood on the very threshold of that awful opening, dense clouds of vapor beating warmly against his chilled features.

His goggles fogged at once, blinding him effectively as, with reason staggering under the accumulated stress of starvation and the circumstances of Alden's disappearance, he groped his way a few feet into the vent. With his left hand he pulled up the glasses from his sunken, blood-shot eyes.

"It's warm, by God!" he cried in astonishment as the skin exposed by lifting the goggles came in contact with the air. "Must be some kind of earth-warmed cave."

INCREASINGLY mystified, he caught up his rifle and strode on down the passage, at that moment illuminated by the last unearthly rays of the aurora borealis. A single, dazzling beam played before him like a powerful searchlight, to light a high vaulted tunnel of basalt rocks which were distorted by some long-gone convulsion of the earth into a hundred weird cleavages and faults. For that brief instant he found he could see perhaps a hundred feet down into a high roofed passage, along the top of which poured a tremendous stream of billowing, writhing steam.

"If this doesn't beat all," he murmured; but for all of his apprehension he did not pause. Those bloody splashes bespeaking Alden's pressing need urged him on. "Looks like I'm taking a one way trip into Hell itself. Well, we'll soon see."

Slipping and sliding over an almost impassable array of black rocks and boulders, Nelson fought his way forward, conscious that with every stride the air grew damper and warmer. Soon trickles of sweat were pouring down over his chest, tickling unbearably.

Then all at once the ray of light faded, leaving him immersed in a blackness equalled only by the gloom of a subterranean vault. He stopped and, resting his rifle against a nearby invisible rock, threw back the parka hood and pulled off his gloves. He was amazed to feel how warm the strong air current was on his hands.

"Beats all," he muttered heavily. "I wonder where they've taken Alden?"

MEANWHILE his hands groped through fur garments now wet with melted-snow and ice particles, searching for the catch to open that pocket in which lay a small but powerful electric flashlight, an instrument without which no far-flying aviator finds himself. After a moment's fumbling, his yet stiffened fingers encountered the cylindrical flash and, with a low cry of satisfaction, he drew it forth to press the button.

"Mighty useful. I..." The words stopped, frozen on his lips. Before the parka edge his close cropped hair seemed to rise, and his breath stopped midway in his lungs. Sharp electric shocks shook him, for there, half revealed in the feeble flashlight's glare, was a sight which shook his sanity to the snapping point. Not fifty feet away two eyes, large as dinner plates, with narrow vertical red irises, were trained on him. Rooted to the ground by the paralysis of utter horror, Nelson saw that their color was a weird, unhealthy, greenish white, rather like the color of a radio-light watch dial.

Strangely intense, these huge orbs wavered not at all, filling him with an unnameable dread, while the strong odor of musk assailed his nostrils. The flashlight slipped from between Nelson's fingers and, no longer having his thumb on the button, flickered out.

Helpless, Nelson stood transfixed against a boulder, aware that the strange, musky scent was becoming stronger. Then to his ears came a dry scrabbling as of some large body stealthily advancing. Those horrible, unearthly eyes were coming nearer! Fierce, terrible shocks of fear gripped the exhausted aviator. Then the impulse of self-preservation, that most elementary of all instincts, forced him to snatch up the rifle, to sight hastily, blindly, between those two, great greenish eyes. Choking out a strangled sob of desperation, Nelson made his trembling finger close over the cold strip of steel that must be the trigger.

LIKE a stage trick, the cavern was momentarily lit by a strong, orange yellow glare. Then the Winchester's report thundered and roared deafeningly; coincidentally arose a nerve-shattering scream. An exhalation, foul as a corpse long unburied, fanned his face. Terrified, he flattened to the rock wall as a huge, though dangerously agile body hurtled by with the speed of a runaway horse. Presently followed the sound of a ponderous fall, then a series of shrill, ear-piercing gibberings and squeakings, like those of a titanic rat—squeaks that rang like the chorus of Hell itself. Gradually they grew fainter, while in the darkness the heavy air of the tunnel became rank with the odor of clotting blood.

Nelson remained where he was, shaking like a frightened horse and bathed with a cold sweat.

"Wonder what it was?" he muttered numbly.

He broke off, for in the terrible darkness sounded a low but perfectly audible *thud! thud! thud! thud!*—and also the subtle noise of some rough surface rasping gently over the stone. His nerves crisped and shrieked for relief.

"It's coming again!" he told himself, and ejected the spent cartridge from the Winchester. "No use—it'll get me, but I may as well fight as long as I can."

Even stronger grew the musty smell of blood while that uncanny *thud! thud!* sound continued at regular intervals. Nelson waited, breath halted and finger on trigger, but still the darkness yielded no glimpse of those awful saucer-like eyes.

EMBOLDENED, he stooped and, jerking off his left glove, commenced to grope among the boulders. Somewhere near at his feet the flashlight must be lying. Hoping against hope that its fall had not shattered the bulb, he ran his fingers over the cold, damp stones, every instant expecting to feel the clutch of the unseen monster. How tiny, how puny he was! All at once his fingers encountered the smooth familiar shape of the flash and he raised it cautiously through the darkness. Patiently he shifted the Winchester to his left hand in order to set the flashlight on the top of a flat rock, pointing it as nearly as he could determine in the direction from whence came those ominous, stealthy sounds.

"Guess I'll switch on the light," he decided, "and trust to drop whatever it is before it reaches me."

Taking a fresh grip on his quivering nerves, Nelson cautiously cocked the .38-55, cuddled the familiar stock to his shoulder. He sighted, then with his right hand pushed down the catch lever of the flashlight.

Instantly a dazzling white beam shot forth to shatter the gloom. The hair on the back of Nelson's hands began itching unbearably, while the cold fingers of madness clutched at his brain, for the sight which met his eyes all but bereft him of his wavering sanity. There, belly up, across a low ridge of basalt, lay a hideous reptile, which in form faintly resembled an enormous and fantastic kangaroo. Its scabby belly was of the unhealthy yellow of a grub, a hue which gave way to a leaden gray as the wart-covered skin reached the back. Two enormous hind legs, each thick as a man's torso and each equipped with three dagger-like talons, struck out in helpless fury at the air, while a long, lizard-like tail threshed powerfully back and forth, scattering ponderous boulders right and left as though they had been marbles. The flashlight being trained as it was, the monster's head and forequarters were invisible, all save two very much smaller and shorter front legs which, like the hinder ones, clawed spasmodically.

"The D.T's!" gasped Nelson, conscious that he was trembling like an aspen. He suppressed a wild desire to laugh. "Yes, I've gone crazy!"

HE glanced downwards and leaped swiftly back, for, creeping over the stones towards his fur outer boots, meandered a wide rivulet of bright scarlet blood. From its surface rose small curling feathers of steam which, drifting towards the tunnel's roof, merged with that gray, vaporous current flowing steadily towards the sunless Arctic expanse outside.

It took Nelson a long five minutes or more to sufficiently recover his equilibrium for action. All he could do was to stare at that grotesque, gargoyle-like creature as it writhed in leisurely and persistent death throes.

"Guess I winged it all right! My God, what a nasty beast! Looks like one of those allosaurs I read about in college. It couldn't be, though—that tribe of dinosaurs died out five million years ago."

Cautiously he scrambled around among the high black stones, casting the search light beams before him and holding the Winchester always ready in his hand while trying to recall snatches of palaeontology studied at college long years ago.

"Yes, it must be a survival of one of the carnivorous dinosaurs," he decided. Then he paused, increasingly conscious of that steady thudding noise. What was causing it?

AT last he found himself standing in front of the creature's gigantic and repulsive head which lay limp over a blood bathed stone, huge jaws partially open, and serrated rows of wicked, stiletto-sharp teeth gleaming yellowly in the flashlight's rays. The head in shape was bullet-like, ending in a blunt nose as big as a bushel basket and in two prominent nostrils. The green, lidless eyes were still somewhat open, shining faintly, and seemed to follow his movements, but the steaming blood poured with the force of a small hose from between triple row of bayonet-like teeth that curved inward like those of a great shark, to splash and bubble freely to the rock floor and to dribble horribly over the warty, gray hide.

Then Nelson discovered an amazing fact. About the great scaly neck, thick as a boy's waist, was fastened a ponderous collar, set with short, sharp spikes.

Nelson gasped. "What in hell!" he cried. "This damn thing's somebody's property!" His mind, staggered at the thought of dealing with a race that could and would domesticate such a hideous monster. "Well, it's no use standing here," he muttered, wiping the sweat from his eyes. "This isn't getting poor Alden away from those devils."

Thud...thud! In the act of turning he paused, and listened once more. Then he discovered to his amazement that the heart of the apparently dead reptile was still beating strongly. He could even see the yellow skin of its belly rise and fall. The effect was grotesque, uncanny.

"Of course," muttered the shaken aviator, "I'd forgotten a reptile's ganglions will keep on beating for hours, like that shark we killed off Paumotu. Its heart didn't stop for five hours."

LEAVING the slain allosaurus behind, the aviator limped onwards, doggedly following a trail which wound down, ever onwards, into the depths of the earth. Gradually the air became so filled with steam that he stripped off his fur jumper and trousers. Clad in a khaki flannel shirt, serge trousers and shoepacks, he paused long enough to count his cartridges, and found there were just fourteen. Hell! Not very many with which to venture into an unknown abyss. He distributed them in his pockets, and, somewhat relieved of the weight of the fur suit, took up his advance, playing the flashlight ahead of him as he went.

"Poor Alden," he thought. "I wonder if he's still alive?"

With every moment expecting to stumble over the mangled corpse of his friend, he hurried on, making far better time over the cavern floor. However, soon even the lighter clothing commenced to feel somewhat oppressive.

"It must be the earth's heat," he muttered under his breath, while the steam clouds rolled by him like ghostly serpents. "Guess the crust is very thin here—something like Yellowstone. Probably I'll find some thermal springs ahead."

Just as he spoke the tunnel took a sudden, sharp turn to the right. He scrambled around the bend to stand abruptly petrified, for with the suddenness of lightning a flood of dazzling orange-red light sprang into being. Momentarily it blinded him, and then revealed strange, almost incomprehensible scenes. It appeared that two short shafts of incandescent flame roared through transparent columns of glass on either side of the passage some fifty yards or more in the distance. Subconsciously Nelson realized that these columns began and ended in stonework that was smooth and well joined.

AS his eyes became accustomed to the glare he distinguished beside each light pillar two bronze doors, some eight feet high and semicircular in shape. These had been evidently pulled back to expose the lights. Then his breath stopped in his throat, for there, standing beside them, was a gleaming group of six or eight of the strangest creatures Nelson could ever have imagined. They were men—there was no mistaking that—men of normal size, but they were so helmeted and incased in a curious type of armor that for a moment he believed them gargoyles.

Quite motionless he stood, clutching tightly the cold barrel of the Winchester in a spasmodic-like grip and staring up at those two watch-towers, which were built like gigantic swallows' nests into sheer rock wall. He could see the warriors stationed there, peering curiously down at him from the depths of heavy, bronze helmets—helmets which in shape much resembled those of an ancient Grecian hoplite, for the nose guards and cheek pieces descended so low as to completely mask the features of those strange guards. For crests these helmets bore exquisitely wrought bronze dolphins, with brilliant blue eyes of sapphire. But what fascinated Nelson most was the curious armor they wore. Beneath breast plates of polished bronze, these strange warriors wore what seemed to be a kind of chain mail—yet it was not that, for the texture had more the appearance of some heavy but pliant leather, finished with a metallic surfacing.

Suddenly the spell of mutual amazement was broken, for a tall warrior in a formidable breast plate that glittered with diamonds and seemed altogether more ornate than the rest, clapped a short brass horn up to his lips and blew a single long, piercing note. At once there appeared on the tunnel's floor, not a hundred yards from the startled aviator, a rank of perhaps twenty soldiers or more, accoutred exactly like those he beheld by the light boxes. They came scrambling over the boulders, their shadows grotesquely preceding them. In their hands were long shafted spears, and on their left arms rectangular shields, charged with a lively dolphin in the act of swimming. There were some of them, though, who held short hoses in their hands, hoses that sprouted from tight brass coils strapped to their broad shoulders.

AGAIN the commanding figure aloft raised the horn. From the tail of his eye Nelson caught the gleam of metal in the orange glare. While a blast, harsh as the scream of a fire siren, echoed and re-echoed eerily through the passage, there appeared a fresh detachment. Nelson shrank back in horror, for these bronze-armored warriors led, at the end of a powerful chain, two more of those huge, ferocious allosaurs, exactly like the one he had slain but a short while back.

Like a formation of well-regulated automatons, the hoplite rank opened up to permit the passage of those repulsive, eager monsters, then closed up again and halted, spears levelled before them in the precise manner of an ancient Grecian phalanx, while the men with those curious hose-like contrivances ran out to guard the flanks.

"I'm done for now," thought Nelson as he threw off the Winchester's safety catch. "I suppose they'll turn those nightmares loose on me."

He was right in his assessment. For all the world as though they led war dogs, the keepers in brazen armor advanced, the dull metallic clankings of their accoutrement clearly discernible above the sibilant hiss of their hideous charges, which hopped along grotesquely like kangaroos, using their long and powerful tails as a counterpoise.

Then the officer watching from the left hand swallow's nest shouted a hoarse, almost unintelligible command, whereupon one of the keepers raised his right hand in a sharp gesture that instantly flattened the incredible monster to earth, exactly like an obedient bird dog.

As in a fantastic dream Nelson watched in horror as one of the armored guardians unsnapped the hook of the powerful chain by which his allosaurus was secured. Then, whistling sharply, he clapped his hands twice and pointed straight at the motionless aviator. The creature's green white eyes flickered back and forth for a moment, and a chill, colder than the outer Arctic, invaded Nelson's breast as those unearthly eyes came to rest upon him.

MEANWHILE the other allosaurus remained crouched, whining impatiently for its keepers to cast it loose.

Fixing burning eyes upon the American, the foremost keeper threw back his head. "Ahre-e-e!" he shouted. Instantly the freed allosaurus arose, balanced its enormous bulk, then commenced to leap forward at tremendous speed, clearing fifteen or twenty feet with each jump and uttering a curious, whistling scream as it bore down, a terrifying vision of gleaming teeth and talons.

Shaking his head and warding off the formidable paralysis of despair, Nelson whipped up the Winchester and, as before, sighted squarely between those blazing, gem-like eyes. When the huge monster was but twenty feet away from him he pulled the trigger and fired. The sharp report thundered and banged in the cavern like the crash of a violent summer storm. In mid-air the ghastly carnivore teemed to stagger. Its tail twitched sharply as in an effort to recover its lost balance. Then, quite like any normal creature that is shot through the head, it lost all sense of direction and made great convulsive leaps, around and around, clawing madly at the air around it, bumping into the rock walls and uttering soul-shaking shrieks of agony. Like a gargoyle gone mad it reeled back towards the startled rank of spearmen. As it came, Nelson saw the second allosaurus rear itself backwards and, balanced on its tail, strike out with powerful hind legs as its maddened fellow drew near.

Like deadly razors the great talons ripped through the vulnerable belly of the dying allosaurus, grossly exposing the gray-red intestines as the stricken creature streaked by, snapping crazily at the empty air.

A single mighty sweep of the monster's massive tail crushed five or six of the panic-stricken keepers and guards, strewing them like broken and abandoned marionettes out among the stones. Hissing and most obviously terrified, the second dinosaur dumbly watched the dying struggles of its mate; then, obedient to a terrified shout from its keepers, wheeled about to join in a frantic rout of the spearmen, who, casting aside shield, spear and brass coil, fled for their very lives in the direction of those invisible passages through which they had appeared.

CHAPTER TWO

NO LESS amazed and alarmed than those vanished soldiers, Nelson remained rooted to the ground, conscious that in the swallow's nest overhead there remained only the officer—a tall, broad shouldered man with golden beard showing from under the cheek pieces of his helmet. Across the body of the still writhing monster their glances met. Nelson could see by the light of those strange pillars of fire that the other's eyes were blue as any Norseman's. Leaning far out over the stone parapet the other stared down upon the aviator from the depths of his jewelled helmet in a strange mixture of curiosity and awe.

Suddenly Nelson's nerves snapped and he shook a trembling fist at the martial figure above.

"Go away!" he shrieked, and reeled back on the edge of collapse. "Go away, you damn phantom! You're driving me crazy—crazy, I tell you!"

The other suddenly stiffened, then turned and, uttering a hoarse shout, vanished, leaving the noiseless and apparently heatless pillar of fire flaring steadily.

Recovering somewhat, Nelson set his teeth, advanced toward the nearest corpse, stooped and regarded him who lay there, with bronze helmet fallen off.

"It's a man and not a ghost," he murmured as his finger encountered flesh that was still warm. "Red headed too, or I'm a liar. Now what in hell is all this?"

For all his bewilderment he began to feel better and his swaying reason became steadier. "Bronze, bronze—nothing but bronze," the aviator told himself as he further examined the scattered equipment. "Evidently these fellows don't know the use of iron or steel."

WITH increased curiosity he bent over another splendidly built dead man who lay with back broken and sightless eyes staring fixedly onto the steam current meandering silently along the cavern's roof. From the fallen man's wide belt were slung half a dozen curious weapons that looked not unlike potato mashers, except that they were bronze headed and had what appeared to be wooden handles.

"Hmmm," he commented, "kinda like the grenades the Boche used in the late lamented. Wonder what the devil these are?"

Suddenly his ear detected the sound of a footstep and, on looking swiftly up, he beheld that same yellow bearded officer who had directed the attack. This strange being had taken off his ponderous helmet to carry it in his left hand, while his right was held vertically in the immemorial sign of peace. On he came with powerful martial strides, a brilliant green cloak flapping gently behind him and the jewels in his brazen armor glinting like so many tiny colored eyes. The stranger was indeed handsome, Nelson noticed—and then he received perhaps the greatest shock of the whole chimerical adventure. The gold bearded man halted some twenty feet away, smiled and spoke in a curiously inflected but perfectly recognizable voice.

"Welcome to the Empire of the Atlans. Prithee, Wanderer, what be thy name?"

For a long moment Nelson was entirely too taken back to make a reply. Desperately his already perplexed brain tried to comprehend. Here was a handsome six-footer, dressed in the arms of an ancient race, speaking English of the seventeenth century!

AS AT a phantom, he regarded the stalwart, faintly ominous figure, from heavy leather sandals to bronze greaves, thence to wide belt from which dangled more of those most curious grenadelike objects. His glance paused on the officer's beautifully wrought bronze cuirasse or breast-plate, which showed in relief an emerald scaled dolphin and trident. These, Nelson decided, must be the various national emblems of this incomprehensible nation.

Then their eyes met, held each other a long moment until the tall officer's features, disfigured by a long red scar across the jaw, broke into a hard smile.

"Hero Giles Hudson begs thy pardon," he said, "but methought thou spoke in the language of Sir Henry Hudson, my ancestor?"

"Sir Henry? Sir Henry Hudson?" stammered Nelson incredulously. "The old explorer whose men turned him adrift? So that's the reason you're talking embalmed English!" In desperation his weary brain strove to understand.

"I know naught," replied the other with a grave smile, "save that the founder of our royal line spoke what he called English. He came from the Ice World to rule wisely over Atlans. He was the greatest Atlantean of history."

"Atlantean?" echoed Nelson, while his mind groped frantically in the recess of his memory. "Atlans, Atlantis!" A great light broke upon him. "The lost Atlantis! Great God!" Had he stumbled upon a remnant of that powerful people whose fabled empire had been drowned ten centuries ago in the cold waves of the Atlantic?

"AYE," the yellow haired warrior continued as though reading his thoughts, "long centuries ago this valley was peopled by those who escaped the great cataclysm which ended the mother country. Later came another race, barbarian wanderers like thyself." He bowed for all the world like a courtly English gentleman. "But methinks thou art in need of food and sustenance?"

"You bet I'm hungry. I'm starved," was Nelson's emphatic reply. "I'm one short jump of starvation and the D.T.'s. But hold on just a minute," he cried. "I'm looking for a friend of mine. He went by here, didn't he?"

"Aye." A crafty expression Nelson did not like crept into Hero Giles Hudson's face as he solemnly inclined his head.

"For the nonce, fair sir, thy companion is hale and sound. I beg your patience."

With a quick gesture the Atlantean raised his dolphin-shaped horn and blew a series of short blasts while Nelson, in sudden alarm, cocked his rifle and brought it in line with the other's chest. The glittering officer saw the motion, but made no effort to move from the line of sights.

"Thy gesture avails naught," said he with stiff courtesy. "When Hero Giles gives his word, it stands good though Heliopolis and the Empire of the Atlans fall."

One by one half a dozen spearmen appeared, all obviously very frightened and only moved by an apparently Spartan discipline. Quite promptly they saluted, whereupon the Hero—as his title appeared to be—uttered a number of brief commands in some guttural language entirely unintelligible to the dazed aviator.

PRESENTLY a strange column appeared, composed of some fifteen or twenty disarmed men marching between a double rank of heavily equipped hoplites. As they drew near, they clasped imploring hands and evidently begged for mercy from the stern, tight jawed figure at Nelson's side. Contemptuous and unhearing the prisoners' piteous pleadings and lamentations, Hero Giles scowled upon them and deliberately turned his back.

"What are they?" inquired Nelson, vaguely alarmed. "Enemies?"

"Yes." There was a certain bitter savagery in the speaker's voice. "These are the dauntless defenders of Atlans who ran at the report of thy weapon. Presently they die."

It was useless to interfere. The horrified aviator knew it and watched with compassionate eyes while the condemned soldiers were ranged in a single, white-faced line. They remained silent now, seeming to have found courage now that hope was dead.

Upon brief command from a subaltern, the guards wheeled about and retreated perhaps twenty yards down the passage. There they halted, glittering eyes peering through the slots in their helmets to fix themselves upon the rigid prisoners who stood numbly resigned to death.

With surprising speed each member of that weird firing squad detached a brazen grenade from his belt, then threw back his arm in exactly the same attitude as a bomb-throwing doughboy. Then there came a short, sharp command and some fifteen or twenty grenades bobbed through the air to crash on the stones at the feet of the victims.

HIS head swimming with repulsion at the grotesque slaughter, Nelson beheld a curious sight. It seemed that from the broken grenades appeared a yellowish green vapor which sprung *of its own accord* upon the silent upright rank! In an instant it settled like falling snow upon the doomed soldiers. For a breathless fraction of a second they stood, eyes wide with horror, then collapsed, kicking and struggling as men do under the influence of gas.

"Horrible!" gasped Nelson. "What was in the bombs?"

"A vapor," explained Hero Giles shortly. "A fungus vapor which, falling upon exposed flesh, instantly invades the blood and multiplies by the millions. See..." He pointed to the nearest dead man and Nelson, with starting eyes, watched a yellowish growth commencing to sprout from the dead man's nostrils. Swiftly the poisonous mould threw out tiny branches, spreading with astounding rapidity over the skin until, in less than a minute after the grenades had exploded, the whole tumbled heap of dead were covered with a horrible yellow green fungus growth.

"Thou seest?" Hero Giles demanded. "Powerful, is it not? It is against the fungus vapor we wear this body armor made from the skin of a small lizard which inhabits our mountains."

Shocked and appalled, Nelson watched the retreat of the solemn, silent execution party.

Other soldiers fell to unconcernedly stripping their fallen comrades of equipment; then, to Nelson's horrified surprise, two hideous allosauri reappeared, shepherded by some six or eight keepers. Once the horrible creatures were released, they pounced upon the dead and, snarling horribly, commenced to rend and devour the corpses.

TOO SHAKEN to comment or to make the protest he knew to be futile, Nelson followed the stalwart English-speaking officer into a bronze door set in the cavern wall and up a short flight of stairs into what appeared to be a guard room, where food and wine were immediately set before the famished aviator.

"Yea," Hero Giles was saying as he set down a beautiful goblet and wiped the last traces of wine from his beard, "we will soon o'ertake thy friend. He was but little hurt, and thou wilt assuredly join him in judgment before our great Emperor, Altorius XXII, at Heliopolis, our capital."

"Heliopolis?" mumbled Nelson, his mouth full of delicious stew that seemed to be made of veal. "Heliopolis? How far away is it?"

"A hundred leagues more or less," the other smiled. "Almost a third of the distance up this great valley."

"One hundred leagues! Three hundred miles! Then we won't be there for several days."

The Hero's deep, rather ominous laughter rang out in the little rock hewn chamber. "Days?" he jeered. "Days? Art thou mad? In two hours from the time we board the tube-road thou shalt learn thy fate from his Serene Highness."

"What!" Nelson's sunken and blood-shot gray eyes widened, while his jaw dropped incredulously. "One hundred leagues in two hours? As I remember there are about three miles to a league, so a hundred leagues in only two hours means one hundred and fifty miles an hour! Why, that's utterly impossible! The Twentieth Century Limited doesn't go half so fast."

Several enormous emeralds set into the other's bronze cuirasse glittered softly and the Hero's cold blue eyes hardened as his hand sought the grenade belt.

"Impossible? Dost doubt my words, sirrah?" With an effort he controlled himself. "Nay, thou shalt see for thyself ere long. The tube-road runs from Heracles to Heliopolis. Thou canst trace its course on this map here on the wall."

"The dog-born devils of Jarmuth have no such means of travel," continued the Atlantean, with a touch of smug pride that reminded Nelson of a small town Middle Westerner speaking of the "rightest, tightest little town to the west of the Mississippi."

Nelson found it extremely weird to be sitting there in a heavy armchair, drinking a very good red wine with a fierce armor-clad warrior who wore sandals, sword and a war cloak such as might have graced the limbs of Alexander of Macedon. But with the food and rich warm wine, he felt blood, strength and self-confidence pouring back into his weary body. "Jarmuth?" he inquired. "What is Jarmuth?"

At his question the domineering, predatory face across the table darkened and the scar on his cheek flamed red as a scowl of hatred gripped Hero Giles' visage.

"Jarmuth!" snarled the Hero, and his great hand closed like a vise. "Jarmuth! A nation of treacherous, gold-adoring cannibals, whose countless hordes, spawned in the hot lowlands, ever threaten our frontiers. I tell thee, Friend Nelson, the dog-sired Jereboam will not rest until mighty Heliopolis lies in a heap of smoking ashes."

"Evidently," thought Nelson, taken aback at the other's apparent vehemence, "this lad's English only in speech. I guess he's all Atlantean outside of that."

WARMING TO A fiercer pitch, the other fixed his guest with a steady, smoldering gaze. "Jarmuth lies beyond Apidanus, which is the boiling river, and is the home of a savage horde whose horrid rites in Jezreel, the capital, stink as an unholy offense to Saturn and the High Gods! Why, mark you," the warrior prince continued, interrupting his tirade to gulp a goblet of wine, "five years ago, by treachery, they seized the beauteous Altara, the sister of our most gracious

Emperor, and upon the annual feast of Beelzebub, that vile demon they worship, the dark dogs would have sacrificed and devoured her, according to their rites, had not our Emperor dispatched a ransom of six fair maidens to take her place.

"Every year since then Jereboam has exacted that same tribute. Every year their princes and priests gorge themselves on the tender white flesh of our fairest and noblest maidens. But this tribute must end! The augurs have told us so. Help will come from the Ice World." Hero Giles brought crashing down on the table a brawny fist, on whose wrist was fixed a bright, gem-studded bracelet.

Horror-stricken, Nelson nodded.

"It is for this alone," continued the Hero somberly, "that thy life and that of thy friend have been spared."

"So? I didn't notice," broke in Nelson, "that you particularly went out of your way to preserve my health a while back."

The heavy golden head shook slowly and a grim smile played about those thin cruel lips. "Nay, but I could have had thee slain. Come, as we go to the tube-road I'll show thee how much thou liest in the hollow of this, my hand." He thrust out a broad, powerful palm. "Forget not, fair sir. At any moment I or my Imperial Master may choose to close that hand."

"Perhaps, perhaps," stated Nelson, feeling it imperative to keep up his pose of independence. "But it might just happen, possibly, that your hand would close on a porcupine, and so far from hurting the porcupine it would be your hand that would be hurt."

"Sirrah!" The Atlantean sprang to his feet and one hand shot to the grip of his ponderous, bronze sword; but even more quickly Nelson snatched up his rifle, a thin smile playing on his lips.

"Drop it," he snapped. "Control yourself, or I'll plug you like that allosaur. Be reasonable, can't you? We both want something, and perhaps can help each other gain it."

THE taut, menacing figure in armor relaxed and, with a gentle clank of accoutrement, Hero Giles resumed his seat.

"Prithee pardon me," he apologized ungraciously. "I was ever a hot-head and there is quite obviously very much in what thou sayest. We wish to force an end to this annual tribute—if not to regain our beloved Altara. And thou..." His heavy, golden eyebrows shot up. "...and thou, what dost thou wish for?"

Nelson lowered the menacing barrel. "I want the return of Richard Alden, free passage back to that spot where he was captured and plenty of food and help should we need it. If I aid you in one, you must promise me in the other."

"Aye," returned the other with a doubtful tone in his voice. "But I myself can pledge naught save thy immediate safety. 'Tis for our Imperial Majesty to say whether both thou and thy friend shall live, or whether ye shall feed our war dogs. Come now, we must go to Heliopolis."

Picking up his heavy, bronze helmet the Atlantean prince set it squarely on the top of his yellowish head and waited impatiently for Nelson to down the last swallow of his wine. Then, with a quick swirl of his greenish cloak, he vanished through the rock wall, closely followed by a singularly distracted and alarmed aviator.

CHAPTER THREE

A BRIGHT yellow glare steadily increased to mark the end of the tunnel down which the two had progressed; then, with the sharp abruptness of a hand-clap, there resounded a loud challenge in that unintelligible Atlantean language, above which the hiss of steam could be loudly heard.

Instantly the Atlantean prince strode forward, a commanding figure. Momentarily his helmet and the dangling grenadelike bombs were sharply outlined against that unearthly yellow light. He raised his hand and dropped it, palm outward, to his chin in what must have been a salute. The hissing sound of steam then faded into silence.

Followed at a respectful distance by a pair of silent, bronze-helmeted hoplites, Nelson and his guide descended a narrow stair, which broadened at the base. It was a very long staircase composed of perhaps two or three hundred steps which were occasionally interrupted by wide stone terraces. On these level spaces were fixed what appeared to be enormous field guns of glittering brass. They were similar, yet somehow oddly dissimilar, to the great guns Nelson had seen in France.

"Behold, oh Wanderer," Hero Giles declaimed impressively, "the lands of Atlans and Jarmuth!"

It was a weird landscape that met Nelson's half-unbelieving gaze, a landscape green with that brilliance peculiar to spring meadows, lying beneath the same deep blue sky that overarched the surrounding barren ice fields which hemmed in this astounding valley.

A slight smile played over Hero Giles' thin lips as he watched the amazed aviator.

"The splendor of our country must indeed astound thee," he observed, "having come from the dreary fastness of the outer Ice World. But come; we are now to pass the great retortii guarding the entrance into the valley."

Nelson's eyes then turned again to the weapons that so oddly resembled field guns. He examined them closely, inspecting them narrowly for the differences he knew must exist between them and the artillery that had thundered during the War of the Nations.

The chief difference lay in the mounting of these starkly beautiful weapons. They seemed to be fixed on a movable pivot set into the coal black rock itself. Like modern artillery, these curious pieces of ordnance bore a bronze shield to protect their crews, through which projected the long and very narrow barrels of the guns. Grouped like cannoneers about their piece stood various red-crested Atlantean artillerymen. At a glance Nelson recognized the difference in their equipment from that of the spearmen behind them. These former bore no shields, no swords or bombs, but wore that same kind of leather body-armor which graced the powerful limbs of Hero Giles. Their helmets, too, were different: only the dolphin crest with a tuft of red feathers spouting from it bore any resemblance to those of the infantry, and, moreover, the artillerymen's eyes were shielded by goggles with thick blue lenses.

AS the Hero approached, officers among them saluted, then sank on one knee with head humbly bent.

"Rather odd looking guns," commented Nelson. "I'm not much of an artilleryman, but I'm wondering how you take up the recoil?"

The Atlantean's laugh, which had always reminded his guest of the loud purr of a tiger, rang out suddenly. "Why, marry, my good sir, there is no recoil! These guns do not use that powder which Sir Henry, founder of our line, did speak of. Thou wouldst see one fired?"

His curiosity immeasurably piqued, Nelson nodded, whereupon the Atlantean wheeled about and barked a brief command. With truly Prussian precision, the artillerymen sprang to their posts, some to a series of levers which sprouted from the rock platform without any apparent connection, and some to wheels and gauges of varying size that clustered in bewildering intricacy about the breech of the great brass gun.

"Markest thou that tree yonder, on the ledge of the valley?" The Atlantean's blunt outstretched finger indicated a towering pine sprouting from among a mass of reddish volcanic rock at the rim of that new world.

"Yes, I see it, but—" Nelson was astounded. A pine tree in the upper Arctic! That alone was sufficient cause for amazement. From a stiff red-plumed gun captain issued a brief series of commands which set the wonderfully drilled crew to silently adjusting their training and elevating mechanism. Click! Clack! Sis-s-s-s!

ALL up and down the vast staircase other gun crews stood watching. Nelson saw their weird, bluish goggles raised to that platform where, for all the world like a coast defense howitzer, the great cannon swung majestically about on the ponderous, brazen column which seemed to support it. Gradually the muzzle was elevated, then traversed a few feet, to finally come to a halt.

"Jakul, a Hero!" shouted the gun captain, his hand raised to Hero Giles.

"Thou art ready, Friend Nelson?" he inquired in tolerant amusement. "Mark well yon pine tree!"

"Storr!"

Nelson saw one of the armored cannoneers bend forward, firmly grasp a short lever with both of his hands. In anticipation of a terrific report, the aviator pressed fingertips to his ears. There followed not a thundering crash, but a curious, eerie, high-pitched scream, rather like that of a fire siren. There was no smoke! Nelson's incredulous eyes sought the muzzle of the gun and detected issuing from it what appeared to be a thin, white rod. This shimmering stream of silver shot straight towards the pine tree, gradually and steadily widening, giving off feathery billows of steam. In a fraction of a moment the target was completely veiled from sight in a furious pall of clouds which, to Nelson's great astonishment, did not dissipate nor condense with the speed of ordinary steam.

"Nava!"

With impressive suddenness the screaming sound faded, leaving a sort of stunned silence on the gun platform. The gunners stalked back to their original stations.

SLOWLY, reluctantly, the mist enveloping the pine tree cleared away and Nelson felt a chill creeping up his spine. The pine was a good three hundred yards away, yet now it sagged limp to earth, stripped of bark, twigs and needles, only the bright yellow trunk and major branches remaining.

"That tree was a good two feet thick," mused the astounded aviator, "yet the steam gun bent it like a sapling. Good heavens! What would it do to a man?"

"What thinkest thou of our retortii?" The Atlantean's beard glinted like metal as he shook with a grim, nearly silent laughter. "These great retortii can shoot half a league and will blast any living thing in their path. I tell thee, friend Nelson, the discharge of even a small retortii will strip the flesh from a man's bones as a peasant strips the husk from an ear of corn!"

"Fearful, terrible!" was Nelson's awed comment. "Is there no defence against them?"

"Of course." The Hero's green feather-crested helmet gleamed with a nod. "Was there ever an instrument of war that had not its defence? Yea, we have the blue vapor to shatter steam particles—it is called the blue maxima. Thou wilt presently see some of our troops armed with it."

"But where does this steam come from? How is it generated?" These two were the first of a host of questions which trembled on Nelson's lips.

"The steam," replied the Atlantean, "comes from the earth. We compress it many times, then feed it into our retortii. Without the heat of Mother Earth and our flame suns we would all perish. Steam is our motive power, our defence and our enemy!"

He flung his hand towards the vast valley that lay stretched before them. It was hemmed in on either side by colossal breath-taking mountain ranges, whose caps shone and glittered with an eternal snow.

"Some foothills! They must rise all of 25,000 feet from the valley floor," decided the aviator, "and I should imagine this valley is a good mile below sea level. Yes! That must be it: this nightmare country lies in a huge geographical fault—something like the Dead Sea."

MILE AFTER mile he could see fertile green land stretching away toward some low undulating hills on the distant horizon. Atlans was very thickly settled—that he recognized at once—for the terrain was divided and then sub-divided into a vast checkerboard, such as he had seen while in France and Germany, while terraces, green with produce, had been laboriously gouged out of the frowning mountain sides.

Then his eye encountered the source of that curious amber light which pervaded the whole valley. A titanic flaming gas vent spouted like a cyclopean torch from the peak of a nearby mountain. Its steady, subdued roar struck Nelson's ear as he turned away his eyes, for the glare was too intense to be long endured. Further down the valley were two more such incandescent vents, shooting their flaming tongues boldly into the sky, warming the air and casting that rich, amber radiance over all.

"That is Mount Ossa nearest us," the Atlantean's voice came as though from a long distance. Victor Nelson was simply too staggered, too unspeakably amazed to register the fact of the Hero's proximity. "Below are Pelion and Jilboa, which, with Jabor, the greatest of all the flames, illuminate and warm the valley."

Nelson's eye, trained to be all observant, ranged far and wide, noting the presence of many lacy, frothing geysers which spouted at varying intervals. There were, also, many steaming ponds and waterfalls which sprang in smoky confusion from the rock palisades to either side.

NEARER at hand he could distinguish a number of huge stone structures, evidently forts and public buildings. Strategically placed all about were more of those terrible brass retortii, gleaming dully under the incandescent glare of the flame sun.

"Come," cried Hero Giles with an impatient gesture of his hand, "we must e'en hasten to the tube-road terminal. Word has long since been sent to Heliopolis of thy arrival."

Downwards into the valley, which gradually grew ever warmer and more fertile, the Atlantean led on, explaining a thousand and one details to the astounded aviator. Presently they approached the nearest of the great stone structures and Nelson received yet another shock. In a courtyard, going through strategic drills, was what would correspond to a troop of cavalry in the outer civilized world. In orderly ranks the troopers wheeled, marched, and then counter-marched, their brazen armor twinkling and clashing softly as they carried out their evolutions with an amazing precision. But what further astonished Nelson was the fact that each of these strange troopers bestrode a lithe, long-limbed variety of dinosaur, a good half smaller than the allosauri he had encountered in the tunnel. These agile creatures ran about on their hind legs with astonishing speed, using a long reptilian tail as a balance.

On the back of each trooper was fastened a compact circular copper tank, from which sprouted a flexible metal hose that ended in what looked like a ponderous type of pistol.

In distinction to the red of the artillerymen and the blue of the Hoplites, these curious cavalrymen wore brilliant crests of yellow feathers, and from their lance tips fluttered tiny pennons of that same color.

"They must travel at least as fast as a race horse," decided the aviator after studying the swift evolutions of the scaly chargers. To his ears came the curious dry scrape and rattle of their horny claws on the stone pavement of the drill yard.

He would have lingered to see more, for those grotesque, lizard-like chargers interested him immensely, but Hero Giles beckoned imperiously. So, dropping the Winchester to the hollow of his arm, Nelson followed him into the brilliantly gas-lit depths of the great structure.

EVERYWHERE were red bearded, white skinned soldiers, staring at him with the frank curiosity of children. Powerful, magnificently built fellows they were, all in uniforms of different designs.

The walls about him, Nelson noticed, were covered with really beautiful friezes depicting various warlike scenes in that pure beauty of proportion found only in ancient Grecian temples.

On and on through resounding tunnels, past busy markets and barracks, hurried the two travelers. Then the Atlantean halted before a gracefully arched doorway where stood two hoplites, who immediately lowered spears to bar the passage. At a word from Hero Giles, however, they saluted and fell back in position— immovable, grim guardians.

Inside was a short staircase, beautifully wrought of bronze. Up this flashed the Atlantean's mail-clad body; then he came to a halt under the direct rays of a blinding light.

Nelson, on arriving above, discovered that the chamber was lined with jointless brass about ten feet high and circular in shape. "What's this?" he demanded curiously.

"The terminal of the tube-road. In a moment thou shalt see the great cylinder arrive."

The words were hardly by the Hero's lips when there appeared, noiselessly and amid a great rush of air, a huge metal cylinder that ran upon a sort of truck. It rumbled up to the edge of the platform and from its end a small door was opened.

HERO Giles exchanged a few sentences with an elderly man who appeared to act as control master, then he indicated the glowing doorway of the cylinder.

Firmly clutching his Winchester, Nelson bowed his head and stepped inside, there to discover a luxury he had never anticipated. The interior of the cylinder was brilliantly lit and on both sides were ranged wide divans, strewn with many silken cushions. In a rack nearby were several graceful glass amphora, filled with red and tawny wine.

"The cylinder must be about thirty feet long," the marvelling American told himself, "and about ten feet in diameter. Guess it works on the same principle as the compressed air tubes the department stores use to send change with."

Gingerly he tested the nearest divan and marvelled at the curious softness of what appeared to be a gigantic tiger skin. Meanwhile Hero Giles entered, his stern features even more serious, but with him was a younger man who resembled him not a little.

"Fair brother," said the Atlantean to his companion, "this is he of whom I spoke. Friend Nelson, this is Hero John, my next youngest brother—he, too, speaks the language of the great Sir Henry Hudson."

The metallic clang of the door being shut brought a sharp qualm to Nelson's heart. "What are they doing?" he demanded quickly.

"The menials bolt the door beyond," explained Hero Giles with amused gravity. "In a moment our cylinder will be placed in the dispatching chamber, where steam pressure will be exerted. We shall then be hurled through this vacuum tube-road to Heliopolis, greatest city of Atlans. In an hour we will be there."

Outside sounded the sudden insistent clangor of a gong, and immediately the hiss of steam grew louder. The car shuddered as the hissing rose to an eery scream, then all at once the cylinder leaped forward, nearly hurling Nelson from his seat. He struggled as best he might to gain his equilibrium, for the eyes of the others were on him.

Then, more smoothly, the great cylinder gathered speed and hurtled on through the darkness of the tube-road towards Heliopolis, where Victor Nelson would read the book of Fate.

CHAPTER FOUR

ON the arrival platform at Heliopolis reigned a fierce excitement. Nelson noted countless armed and unarmed warriors hurrying to and fro, desperately intent on reaching their various posts, and snarling ill-temperedly as they elbowed their fellows aside. As soon as they appeared, Hero Giles and his brother became the center of an excited press of gorgeously armored officers.

"Hum!" murmured the aviator under his breath. "Something's happened. Must be a revolution, an earthquake or a Democratic convention in town; these boys seem all steamed up."

Intently he studied the ring of fierce, red bearded faces surrounding his late hosts and gathered that indeed some event of overwhelming importance had taken place. Presently a splendid falcon-eyed old man in a yellow cloak strode up, struggling to control himself. His resemblance to the two Heroes struck Nelson immediately.

"Harken ye," he cried, in that Elizabethan English which appeared to be the hieratic language of the New Atlantis' rulers. "Have ye heard? The dog-conceived sons of Semites have broken the truce! But three measures gone by, a brigade of their mounted podokesons swooped down on this very suburb of Tricca, yea, to the very gates of Heliopolis! The foul man-eating dogs slaughtered royal serfs and burnt two quarters of the suburb to the ground! Moreover, they seized that prisoner…" Nelson's heart gave a great leap at the word. "…whom thou sentest from the mountain passes."

"What!" In two swift strides Nelson was before the gray beard, his blood-shot eyes blazing with a strange light. "What did you say about that prisoner?"

THE old man, who had obviously not noticed Nelson's presence, was thunderstruck to hear him speak in English until Hero Giles briefly explained his presence.

"Yea!" continued the elder, flinging lamentations furiously over his shoulder, "these swine of the Lost Tribes captured him and slew his escort. They have retreated towards the Apidanus, slaying, burning and pillaging as they go."

A sickening, deadly fear gripped the weary aviator. This was too much! Bad as it was to have Richard Alden captured by these weird descendants of a long vanished race, it was far worse to have him fall into the hands of their deadly enemies, the Jarmuthians, decadent survivors of Israel's Five Lost Tribes. The possibility of a rescue now seemed hopelessly and crushingly vague and distant. What could he do now?

In dread despair he glanced about, amazed at the prodigious numbers of scowling men who hurried by, obviously intent upon the commencement of a campaign for revenge.

Then Hero Giles turned his scarred, warlike face, now set in granite lines. "Come, Friend Nelson, my uncle Anthony bids me take thee direct to the presence of His

Serene Splendor, where he lies encamped at Cierum, by the shores of Lake Copias. There he marshals the army of Atlans for a march through the hot country on Jezreel. I tell thee, thou hast come in stirring times. From Heraclea, Thebes, Ys and Mayda will come the Phalanxes. Once and forever we will deal the dogs of Jarmuth a final blow."

VICTOR Nelson never forgot the hours that followed. Issuing at a fast trot from the tube-road terminal, the two Heroes led the way to a vast structure, in which were stabled both the terrific allosauri and the podokesauri, those swift dinosaurs which seemed to serve the Atlanteans as horses. The dreadful hiss and snarl of these monsters resounded in his ears long before the stables came in sight, and that curious musky odor he had noted in the tunnel was sickeningly strong.

Everywhere he read signs of hurried preparations for war. Savage, surly allosauri were led from their stables, one by one, long necks writhing snakelike backwards and forwards. Then their keepers would, after a moment's tussle, secure huge leather muzzles over their gaping jaws, and the huge reptiles would be led waddling along on their hind legs out into a vast courtyard, there to hiss and strike at their nearest fellows.

"Thinkest thou couldst ride a podoko?" inquired Hero John, an anxious look on his handsome, friendly features. "They are difficult to manage—but swift in flight as the birds themselves!"

"I don't know," replied the aviator, "but I'm damn well going to try. If your Emperor can help me rescue Alden, the sooner we get started, the better."

For all his brave resolutions, his heart sank, as the green kilted keeper led forth three podokesauri. Nelson stared curiously at them as, hopping along, they drew near, to bare needle-sharp teeth at him while, brazen stirrups on either side jangled softly against their rough, scaly hides.

In evident high spirits the beasts snuffed the air and pawed with their tiny front legs excitedly, making their sharp talons glisten like polished steel. A bridle dangled from the mouth of each and a ring set in the thick upper lip served as a further means of control.

AT a sharp "*Oya!*" from an old and toothless keeper, the first podoko sank flat to the stone floor like a kneeling camel.

"A sturdy beast," commented Hero Giles, tightening his belt and securing the clasps to the emerald-green war cloak. "Here, Friend Nelson, thou hadst best don a helmet; the podokos on occasion throw back their heads and so might wound thee." So saying, he set foot in stirrup and swung up into a saddle which was built up high in the cantle to correct the sharp downward slope of the reptile's muscular back.

At a signal, Hero Giles' ugly mount rose to its height and shuffled awkwardly sidewise, as the old keeper, his eyes very wide and curious, led forward Nelson's charger.

"Look," said Hero John with a reassuring smile. "The chin strap buckles so—be sure it fits snug, else it will pound on thy head to the podoko's stride. If thou wouldst turn to the left, pull the rein so, to the right so, and if thou wouldst stop, pull strongly on the nose ring;

'tis not so difficult." He laid a friendly hand on Nelson's flannel clad shoulder. "How wilt thou manage thy curious weapon?" he inquired doubtfully. "Perhaps thou hadst best leave it behind."

There was a grim smile on Nelson's weary and wind burned features. "Not on your life, old son! This Winchester and I stick closer together than the Siamese twins."

Nelson thrust his foot into a heavy stirrup, eased his weight into the high peaked saddle and gripped the pommel, for though an excellent horseman, he had no clue as to what motion would ensue. It was wise he did so, for the podoko reared suddenly, almost flinging his rider from the saddle.

IMMEDIATELY Hero John mounted, raised his right hand and dealt his podoko a stinging slap on the fore-shoulder. The great reptile hissed in protest, but commenced to walk off with an awkward, hopping step. Nelson's mount followed suit.

Faster and faster ran the podokos, their long and scale-covered necks stretched far out ahead while their tails lifted correspondingly, much like that of an airplane about to take off.

"Whew! He must be doing all of forty-five," gasped Nelson, while the wind whistled about his ears and snapped madly at the yellow crest of his brazen helmet.

The ride which ensued remained forever fixed in the aviator's memory. Like so many shots from a gun the three podokos darted off out of the stables, past a gate guarded by a battery of retortii, whose red plumed cannoneers sprang to attention as the three strangely assorted riders sped out into the amber, perpetual light of Atlans.

Nelson, on finding his balance, looked about him to receive impressions of immensely tall structures, of pyramids which, like the ziggurats of Sumaria, and Babylon, were surmounted with beautifully proportioned temples.

"Must be at least a million people in this burg of Heliopolis," thought Nelson, easing his Winchester.

Hour after hour they sped along, frequently overtaking detachments of troops. Twice they halted to change mounts, though the podokos seemed quite tireless.

At the end of five hours' furious riding, Nelson beheld a dense white cloud low on the horizon.

"What's that?" he demanded. "Fog?"

"No," Hero John informed him. "Yonder flows the Apidanus, the boiling river. Not far away to the left lies the frontier fortress of Cierum, where is encamped the Emperor, who will sit in judgment upon thee."

Nelson's heart sank. He had been so occupied with his fears for Alden that he had not dwelt upon his own precarious position.

SCARCELY half an hour elapsed, if Nelson's wrist watch were running correctly, before he reached the tremendous, swarming camp of Altorius XXII, Emperor of Atlans. Hero Giles proved to be a powerful talisman, for everywhere officers and men alike saluted respectfully and sank on one knee as he passed.

"Wait here," he snapped, as the podokos sank obediently to the dust. "Brother John, do thou guard

Friend Nelson while I seek permission of His Serene Splendor to bring the Wanderer into the Presence."

Almost immediately the elder Atlantean returned, a frown on his scarred, rather brutal visage. "Come," he muttered, "but I fear for thee, Friend Nelson; His Splendor is in a savage mood—this raid hath stirred his ire beyond all bounds."

"Nothing like cheering up a patient before he goes into the operating room," thought Nelson, and quietly threw off the safety on his Winchester. "Six shots," he reflected. "Well, if I go, I reckon I'll take some damn good company along."

The aviator was led down a long passage, at every ten feet of which was posted an enormous scowling guard, whose spears, retortii and armor were painted a brilliant jade-green. Then a musical, deep-toned gong boomed twice, and Hero Giles halted before an exquisitely wrought door, which, without any apparent propulsion, silently slid back into the massive stone walls, revealing a huge, brilliantly lit circular chamber that was hung with emerald-green hangings. In the center, surrounded by a royal guard of nobles in splendidly jeweled armor, was reared a dais, upon which stood a throne that blazed with the most varied collection of diamonds that Nelson could ever have imagined.

"Down on your face," rasped Hero Giles as, in common with his brother, he knelt and then fell prostrate on the cool black marble floor.

"Damned if I will," murmured Nelson, and remained erect.

BOLT upright, he looked across the interval and found himself staring into the furious eyes of one of the handsomest men he had ever beheld. Gripping his Winchester in a kind of "port arms" position, he stood to attention—by some curious kink of the brain reverting to his military days. And so the two men, different as day and night, faced each other. Altorius XXII clad in robes of scarlet, and a glittering cuirasse that glowed like the evening sun. His yellow head was truly splendid, reminiscent of that of a young Roman Emperor. The hair, like that of the Hudsonian Heroes, was blond, curly and close cropped. Yes, thought the awed but self-contained American, there was something genuinely imperial about the Emperor's aquiline visage, for a high intelligent forehead and piercing blue eyes dominated a strong mouth, which was marred by a decidedly cruel twist at the corners. On him, also, was set the stamp of Sir Henry Hudson's dauntless race.

"Put him is a business suit and a soft gray hat," mused Nelson, "and you would find a dozen like him in any of London's best clubs."

"Down on thy face, sirrah!" Outraged, the Emperor's voice rang like the peal of a brazen trumpet through the great pillared audience chamber. The nearest guardsmen held themselves ready, hand on sword hilt.

"No." Nelson's shaggy black head went back as he found his tongue at last. "No, Your Majesty. In America we have our own way of showing respect for authority. I'm an American and, with all respect, I'll salute you as one."

So saying, his hand flicked up in a sharp military salute to the visor of that Atlantean helmet which he still wore.

"All damn foolishness," he silently told himself. "I feel like the lead in a ten, twenty, thirty melodrama. But I suppose it's got to be done."

THE Emperor's teeth gleamed in a half snarl as he sprang with Jovian wrath to his feet.

"Dog! How darest thou bandy words with us?"

"Have mercy!" hoarsely pleaded Hero John as he lay on the floor. "Have mercy, oh Splendor! He is but an ignorant wanderer from the Ice World."

It appeared that the young Hero was something of a favorite, for the masterful, thunder-browed Emperor checked himself and, still glowering, settled back on the diamond throne.

"Ye have my permission to enter and approach."

Whereupon, Hero Giles arose and, with many black looks at his guest, strode forward to briefly explain his presence.

Nelson felt Altorius' blazing blue eyes search his face.

"Then he whom the dog-born Jereboam captured was thy friend?"

"Yes," replied Nelson with dignity, "my best friend. Alden and I have traveled and wandered all over the world together."

"Over the world? The Ice World?" Altorius seemed interested, for he leaned forward, muscle corded arms very brown against the frosty brilliance of the stones studding his throne. He flipped back a scarlet cloak and bent a searching look on the straight, unafraid figure below.

Impatient to reach a decision, Nelson forebore to amplify the Emperor's assumption that the outside world was all ice and snow.

"Yes," he said, "from the land of America. I've spoken with Hero Giles, Your Majesty's Captain-General."

"So, then, no doubt, he has told you of the law of our country?" Altorius' white teeth shown again in the depths of his short, curling beard.

"Perhaps." Nelson was vague, wishing no further amplification.

"The law of Atlans," pronounced the Emperor with a frown, "states that a stranger must prove his worth to the State, else he must be put to death. Thank thou thy gods that thou hast not fallen into the hands of the Lost Tribes, for assuredly thou would perish miserably, as must thy comrade."

"THAT is the law of Jarmuth?" inquired Nelson, his mind furiously at work.

"Their law states that the stranger within their gates must perish on the altar of Beelzebub, Jarmuth's blood-hungry demon god." A momentary expression of sadness crept into the Emperor's blue eyes and he beat a square, powerful hand on the arm of his throne. "Aye, blood-hungry! Lack-a-day! But yesterday, six of our fairest maidens crossed the boiling river, never to return."

Nelson was about to speak when from outside came the blast of a trumpet. The assembled Atlanteans started, paused, and remained silent, listening intently.

Hero Giles looked up, a light kindling in his deep-set eyes. "Yon was an Israelite trumpet."

As the words left his lips there came a hurried rapping at the portal, whereupon the guards sprang forward.

"Bid them enter." Altorius seemed strangely tense and uneasy.

Quietly the door rolled back as before, revealing an Atlantean whose eyes rolled with alarm. He hurried forward and flung himself on the floor at the Emperor's sandaled feet.

"Harken, oh Serene Splendor! Waiting without is an embassy from his Majesty of Jarmuth. They bear words for thine Imperial Highness."

"Now, by Saturn! Here's insolence—at an hour such as this!" With a furious swirl of his scarlet cloak Altorius leaped to his feet, hand on the ivory handle of his sword, which, to Nelson's amusement was not of bronze, but of good, blue-gray steel.

"I'll bet it's old Sir Henry's original pet sticker," he thought.

"Bring on these dogs of Israel," growled Altorius. "They shall die!"

"Gently, gently, oh Splendor," murmured Hero John. "Our full force is not yet camped on the Plains of Poseidon."

"Nay! Have the rogues flayed alive!" was the advice of the hot-headed elder brother. He, like the Emperor, was scowling and livid with fury.

PRESENTLY there appeared four men, stalwart warriors as totally different in aspect from the Atlanteans as humans might be. The two races were alike only in splendid physical proportions and human figures. They, the Jarmuthians, were black haired and dark skinned, whereas the Atlanteans, with the exception of Sir Henry's progeny, were red headed. Truculently the half naked ambassadors strode over the polished floor, which reflected their rude images. Their hairy chests, arms and legs afforded a sharp contrast to the neat Atlantean nobles, who drew back with expressions of disgust.

"Good God!" gasped Nelson in lively surprise. "A bunch of the boys from Seventh Avenue!"

It was true: each Jarmuthian clearly betrayed his Hebraic origin in huge, fleshy nose and pendulous lower lip, so characteristic of the Semitic race. They were fierce, shaggy fellows, naked from the waist up save for a kind of jointed body armor, reminiscent of a Roman legionnaire's. Their long abundant blue-black hair was either plaited or flowed uncut over splendidly muscled shoulders. Their beards on the other hand were short and frizzed into tight curls, in the Assyrian manner. On each man's head was set a highly polished, pointed casque of copper, surmounted in each instance by the six-pointed star of Solomon. Otherwise the brutal looking emissaries wore nothing but dirty, food-spotted kilts and rough hide sandals secured by thongs.

WITH all the insolence and self assurance of conquerors in the presence of slaves the four jet-eyed ambassadors swaggered up to the diamond throne. Then the foremost briefly inclined his head towards

Altorius in a grudging salute and began to speak in deep, resonant tones.

From that point Nelson could understand nothing of the conversation as it was carried on in the guttural and unintelligible language of that lost realm, but, from time to time Hero John found opportunity to translate an occasional phrase.

Darker and darker grew the brows of the gorgeously attired Emperor and his eagle-visaged Captain-General as they listened to the pompous oratory of the foremost Jarmuthian, and in dark fury more than one Atlantean noble half drew his sword when the speaker fell silent at last.

"He said," the younger Atlantean whispered, "that Jereboam is no longer satisfied with six maidens. Beelzebub demands a further offering of six more damsels to be delivered before the third division of time on the morrow. By Saturn! The insolence of these besotted swine passes all tolerance!"

From the Atlantean Emperor's outraged negative gestures, Nelson surmised that Altorius was making an emphatic refusal and even adding some vicious threat. The foremost Jarmuthian slapped huge dirty hands on armored hips and fell to laughing with an insolence that would have provoked a rabbit.

FORGETTING dignity and self-control, Altorius, in a single tigerish leap sprang from his throne and knocked the mocker senseless with a powerful blow to the jaw. Then, spurning the fallen Jarmuthian with a sandaled foot, the Atlantean fixed blazing eyes upon the three other ambassadors who, nothing daunted, closed up, muttering savagely in their frizzed black beards, while their hands sought the spot where swords would normally have hung.

"Nice right to the jaw," commented Nelson with a slight grin. "He's still English enough to use his fists." He turned to Hero John, who stood with an expression of horror on his comely features. "What caused the row?"

"Verily, our plight is grave indeed. That braggart dog threatened to march on Heliopolis in the first division of morning, and..." Hero John's lips compressed into a hopeless, taut expression. "...our reinforcing phalanxes can never arrive in time to defend Cierum at that hour. Should the defense fail, as it must—since they outnumber us three to one for the nonce—it would cost us many thousands of men to stay the blood-hungry hordes of Jereboam once freed on the great plain."

Like a star shell bursting on a cloudy night came the inception of an idea.

"Here," cried Nelson, "I've an idea! Maybe I can fix a stall until the rest of your boys do a General Phil Sheridan and get here."

Hero John's blue eyes widened uncomprehendingly. "What?" he demanded. "What dost thou propose?"

NELSON'S hand crept to his head, for the unaccustomed weight and heat of the helmet made it itch. "You say these bright boys from over the border want to chow six more girls? Am I right?"

"Yea, oh Friend Nelson, they demand the victims to-morrow morn, else they advance."

"All right." Nelson was thinking fast now, a dreadful vision of Richard Alden stretched for sacrifice on the brass altar of Beelzebub ever floating before his aching eyes. "Tell those Semites that they can have those six girls *if* they can take them away from me."

A puzzled frown creased the younger Hero's brow and he tugged thoughtfully at his scant yellow beard. "Prithee pardon me, but I do not comprehend."

"All right, get this now! Tell the Jarmuthians that they can send six of their biggest and best scrappers, one for each girl. If they can take any one of those girls away from me, they take them all—taking me as well—and we'll all get the works in Jezreel together. But, on the other hand, if I kill their six champions, then Alden is returned unharmed, the six girls come home and the six other girls come back too—and there'll be no more hostages. I don't think they'll agree to or even consider surrendering Your Princess, Altara. I'm sorry I can't accomplish that, too. But if I can stop this annual tribute, it won't be so bad, will it?"

ROUNDER and rounder grew the Atlantean's eyes, and he gaped like a school boy in a side show.

"What sayest thou? Thou alone to overcome six of their best warriors? Nay, but this is folly! Moonshine! What knowest thou of their weapons?"

"Nothing," admitted Nelson, "but I do know Brother Winchester here." He patted the smooth stock. "He's mighty persuasive, properly handled."

"But they are armored! They have the fungus bombs, the light retortii and the javelin!"

"Righto!" agreed Nelson a trifle carelessly, "but you don't know what this old boy can do when he's put to it. Well?"

"By Saturn!" An uncertain ring crept into the Atlantean Prince's voice. "A moment, while I address His Splendor."

"I'm a fool, nothing but a damn fool!" thought Nelson. "Still, it's Alden's only chance—unless the Jarmuthians have got some kind of trick I'm not on to, I ought to stand a fighting chance." Meanwhile Emperor and Captain-General drew to one side, listening to Hero John's impassioned oratory. That the idea met with disapproval, Nelson quietly recognized from the incredulous, even contemptuous, glances Altorius shot at him. Leaving the four sneering Jarmuthians under guard of the nobles, the Emperor came striding impatiently over the inlaid floor.

"What madness is this?" he demanded in a harsh manner. "Dost thou realize what would hang upon thy skill? If thou shouldst fail, our annual hostage for the divine Altara would be twelve instead of six of our maidens. Further, the dog-conceived Jereboam would wax unbearably overweening and insolent. Nay, there is far too much at hazard! Though outnumbered we will give battle in the morning."

"Yes?" demanded Nelson, impatient in his own turn. "A fine chance you'd stand! Why, something less than half of your army is here at Cerium and Hero John tells me that the enemy have massed their entire forces on the salient of Poseidon. Isn't that so?"

ALTORIUS' handsome brow then darkened a bit. "Aye," he admitted, "but our reinforcing corps will come up before the third hour of the third division."

Here Hero Giles broke in and, speaking with the quick, impassioned tones of one whose reactions are violent, pled for confidence in the American. "Nay, fair cousin," he replied, casting a long sidewise glance at the Jarmuthians standing in muttered colloquy with their leader, who had now gotten to his feet and was angrily dabbing the blood dripping profusely from his chin with the rough hem of his yellow kilt-like garment. "I saw with mine own eyes what miracles Friend Nelson doth perform with his curious noise-making retortii. If Jereboam falls upon us ere our staunch regiments are marshaled, then, verily, are we utterly doomed. We really have no choice now but to play for time—and as much time as possible. Harken to the counsel of Hero John! Methinks that this stranger from the Ice World is not a braggart. He will fight well, I suspect. And if he loses he dies horribly—that he knows. The thought will strengthen his arms, and if he wins—!"

Then Nelson broke in firmly, saying, "If I win I must have the word of Your Majesty that Alden and I are to be afforded all help and free passage to that place where your soldiers captured my friend. It that completely understood?"

Altorius' blue eyes shifted and there was a slight hesitation in his manner. Then, coming to a decision, he whirled and extended his hand.

"Good, 'tis agreed," he said. "On my head be it. Have patience while Hero Giles confers with these outlandish dogs."

It was with intense interest that the anxious aviator watched the ensuing conference. He could see the four Jarmuthians listening, dark eyes restlessly flitting back and forth, and their mouths twisted into contemptuous half snarls. Then, as Nelson's offer was made clear, a look of cunning seemed to creep into the eyes of the leader. He asked for clarification of several points, then, being informed of the details, his thick lips parted in an evil, crafty grin.

TAKEN aback somewhat at the suspiciously ready acquiescence of the enemy, Hero Giles turned about. "They agree," he translated, "that, should Friend Nelson be the winner, they will return to their own land, they will forfeit the annual tribute forever and return the other stranger unharmed. They speak fair, but I fear—" He bit his lips in perplexity. "These dogs, who talk with the forked tongues of serpents, plan some snare, some cunning trickery."

"Repeat the terms." Altorius seemed gripped with apparent apprehension, too. "Let everything be clear, concise, and fully understood: at the third division of morning will the wanderer fight six warriors. No more and no less."

This was agreed and reaffirmed. Then, with an insolent, triumphant laugh, the Jarmuthian delegation whirled about and stalked from the room, their dark greaved legs flashing in military unison over the polished floor.

"'Tis done," quoth Hero Giles somewhat gloomily. "The encounter will take place on the plain of Gilboa at the third hour of the third division. And may Saturn help us if thy might fails. Friend Nelson! For then surely will the hordes of Jarmuth despoil us and there will come a desolation and a darkness upon the Empire of Atlans."

CHAPTER FIVE

IT seemed incredibly soon that Victor Nelson found himself striding out from the serrated ranks of the Atlantean army which, drawn up in a rough diamond formation, looked discouragingly small in comparison to that vast sea of helmets twinkling ominously across the plain of Poseidon amid a haze of bright yellow dust which climbed lazily into the breathless heavens. The Jarmuthian army, numbering perhaps sixty or seventy thousand effective troops, lay encamped in a great salient formed by a convolution of the Apidanus and formed the only Jarmuthian tract of the great valley lying south of the boiling river.

Like low-lying snow drifts, the sheen of the enemy tents struck Nelson's eye as he strode over the bright green turf to battle for Richard Alden's life.

"There was something back of those nasty grins of the ambassadors," he reflected. "I wonder what deviltry they're cooking up?"

He glanced at a stalwart Atlantean herald who, nervous in the extreme, clutched his brazen, dolphin-shaped horn and followed in the American's wake together with a sad little company. Weeping, moaning and dressed in plain black robes marched six really lovely girls—they who would perish on Beelzebub's altar if Nelson failed. Bitter were the looks of the guards as they secured the hands of the victims and many the hopeful look cast at the impassive American when they turned back, leaving the helpless girls to their fate.

The ground where the one-sided duel was to take place was marked off by means of little yellow flags on a level plain perhaps a quarter of a mile long and wide. Arriving on the nearest border Nelson briefly motioned the herald to halt.

"Might as well start shooting at the best range possible, and beat their steam throwers," he decided. "Wish to the devil I'd a few more cartridges. Only thirteen shots between me and Beelzeebub's altar in Jezreel, so I'd better not miss. All right, son, toot your horn."

WITH his thumb be gestured the command, whereupon the Atlantean nodded eagerly and, filling his chest, set horn to lips to blow a long, strident note that rang harshly, boldly out over the great plain.

While the note of the challenge rang out, Nelson's eyes turned back to regard the Atlantean array and detected, far in the rear, a huge pillar of dust which must mark the progress of the Atlantean reinforcements. Would they arrive at Cierum in time? Then his eyes sought that spot where Altorius and his staff sat anxiously on their podokos, watching intently the impending struggle. Very clearly the flash of their armor came to him.

"I guess, like the girls back there, they're kind of nervous and jumpy," thought Nelson. "Well, I don't blame them. I've had quieter moments myself."

Having blown three blasts, the Atlantean herald saluted; then, with disconcerting haste, made his way back to the ranks of his fellows some two hundred yards away.

From the Jarmuthian army came an answering blast. Nelson cast a last look on the Atlantean army, breathlessly awaiting the impending duel. There was the allosauri corps on the far left; he could see the chimeric monsters' long, repulsive necks writhing endlessly back and forth through the air as they squealed and tugged strongly at their restraining chains. On the right were stationed perhaps ten thousand podokesons, their slender, yellow-shafted lances swaying like a sapling forest in the distance. In the center were eleven thousand protection infantry, green-crested and armed with compact tanks of blue-maxima vapor, fungus bombs and swords. Behind them, and corresponding to heavy infantry, were ranged some twenty thousand blue-plumed hoplites, eagerly fingering the brazen hoses of their death dealing portable retortii.

NELSON had no time to further study the array, for he whirled about as from the Atlantean army arose a deep, horrified shout. He stood paralyzed, his jaw slack. For there, waddling slowly forward, came the most fantastic huge creature imaginable. Unspeakably repellent and horrible, it stood on short legs thick as mature trees, to tower at least thirty-five feet above the ground at the fore-shoulders! An immense reptilian neck some twenty-five feet long weaved continuously back and forth, while a surprisingly small, bullet-shaped head emitted rumbling grunts.

"Great God!" gasped the horrified aviator, and felt the ground sway under him. "It must be ninety feet long!"

Paralyzed by a dreadful fascination he watched the ungainly, hill-like reptile shuffle ponderously forward and realized that, high on its back, was fixed a small fort, rather like those howdahs or boxes which are fastened to the backs of elephants. Chilled with the nearness of death, Nelson counted six mail-clad warriors in the howdah. Then the true import of the Jarmuthians evil jest struck him with full force.

"Six men, they said. And six men there are—but the treacherous devils mounted them on that walking hillside! Guess Altorius can kiss his six girls good-by right now. Poor Alden! Well, I did my best—a rotten trick."

AT that moment he felt as an ant must feel on beholding the approach of a human. It was terrifying, the inexorable advance of that colossal, fantastic monster. From behind he could hear the infuriated shouts of the Atlantean army. They knew even he could not hope to withstand the murderous onslaught of the beast now entering the duelling space.

On came the diplodocus, its vast warty tail trailing over the ground and raising a heavy column of dust, while its mud smeared sides bore out Hero Giles' statement that here was one of those semi-aquatic titans from the steaming swamps of Jarmuth.

"Hell! Poor Alden's as good as finished now! What a fool I was to think I could save him!"

Obedient to an overwhelming fear, Nelson whirled to flee, then stopped, as, from the depths of his being, a stronger power forbade him to desert his friend to certain death.

"Range two hundred and fifty yards," he estimated, and, whipping up the Winchester, sighted full at the ponderous creature's slimy snakelike head. When the recoil jarred his shoulder, Nelson dropped the barrel an inch or so to watch. Nothing happened. The great beast was advancing as before, its incredibly long neck weaving steadily back and forth as though to sniff the air.

"Hell!"

Struck by a sudden thought, he snatched a cartridge from his pocket and, with that strength which comes to men in their hour of mortal peril, wrenched out the metal-jacketed bullet, to reinsert it backwards into the brass cartridge case.

Meanwhile the vast brute had drawn nearer, crushing flat a young oak in its path as easily as though it had been a wheat stalk.

"Maybe this dum-dum will do some good," panted Nelson. "If it doesn't, nothing will stop it!"

AGAIN he sighted until, finding those small, orange red eyes in line with his sight, he fired. This time the gray-brown monster uttered a titanic bellow of rage, halted, and began shaking its clumsy blunt head.

"Hit it, by God!" exulted Nelson, and seized the momentary respite to slip two fresh cartridges into the Winchester's magazine.

But, to his inexpressible dismay, the monster presently resumed its ponderous progress while the Jarmuthians in the howdah uttered taunting yells that reached him faintly, while the sun flares glinted on their brandished swords and lances. One of them plucked a fungus grenade from his belt and flung it with all his might in Nelson's direction. The missile fell to the earth far short of its destination and seemed to break rather than explode, at the same time expelling that deadly, greenish-yellow vapor which, blown away by a strong wind, fortunately came nowhere near the doomed aviator.

"Oh! You will?"

Nelson sighted swiftly at the grenade-thrower and fired, whereupon the Jarmuthian, some hundred and fifty yards distant, spun crazily about, flung both arms towards the amber-yellow sky and toppled from the howdah, for all the world like a diver in quest of pearls.

From both breathless armies rose a terrific shout. Accustomed as they were to the visible destruction of the retortii, this noisy yet invisible death was appalling.

But Nelson's agonized attention was not on the assembled armies, for nearer came the mountainous diplodocus, its lumbering strides making the howdah sway like a ship in a gale and preventing use of the portable retortii.

NELSON planted both feet, took fresh grip on his waning courage and shot again, this time aiming at a gigantic, black bearded warrior who seemed to be training one of those portable retortii upon him.

Again the Winchester cracked and this time the black bearded man sank from sight back into the howdah, while his companions, uttering vengeful shouts, tossed more fungus bombs at the lone heroic figure barring their progress towards the six bound and shrieking maidens.

Towering thrice as high as the largest African elephant, the diplodocus was now but seventy-five yards away. He had hit it, that Nelson could tell, for a large shower of blood sprayed from the monster's neck. Then, uttering a despairing curse, he sent a shot smacking squarely into the left shoulder, at the base of that mastlike neck with fervent hope of finding the heart. But the heavy bullet bothered the cyclopean reptile no more than a sting of a mosquito.

On, on it came. In another minute it must stamp out Victor Nelson's life beneath feet as large as hogsheads.

"Damn!"

Nelson snapped the ejector lever, throwing out the spent cartridge.

"No use," he whispered, "can't faze that hill of meat! But I might as well kill all of those bloody cannibals I can."

With amazing speed and accuracy he picked off two of the remaining Jarmuthians, whose shining, bronze armor could nowise withstand the wicked impact of modern nickel-jacketed bullets. One of the stricken men for a moment dangled with the last of his strength from one of the chains securing the howdah to the enormous creature's back, then tumbled heavily some forty feet to the earth.

Only two shots more in the magazine—! Nelson suddenly found himself very cool. "Two shots and then—"

He was conscious of that great, snakelike head darting viciously in his direction. A huge, slobbering mouth, studded with teeth a foot long, yawned redly before him like a nightmare incarnate, blotting out consciousness of all else. Then Victor Nelson, fighting to control his strumming nerves, deliberately sighted into a great, orange colored eye, saw the narrow black iris over the Winchester's front sight and knew the huge warty head was not ten feet away.

HE pressed the trigger and never heard the report, but felt the blast of a furnace-hot breath in his face—a breath that stank like the foul reek of burning rubber.

With a detached sense of surprise he saw the eye miraculously and dreadfully disintegrate; then, as the bitter smell of burned cordite stung his nostrils, he sprang violently sidewise to find himself staring up at the howdah, now towering at least forty feet above.

The next several moments were practically indescribable. Horrible roars and bellows, loud as those of a thousand angered bulls, shattered the air. The diplodocus halted, stunned by pain and the partial loss of eyesight; then, its infinitesimal brain becoming gripped with fear, it plunged and lumbered in a sidewise manner, nearly shaking the warriors from the howdah, where they clung for dear life. Nelson was barely able to avoid the sweep of the powerful tail as the diplodocus wheeled about on hind legs, reeled and started blindly back towards the Jarmuthian ranks. Suddenly it stood stock still, shaking with super-elephantine motions. Then, for all the world like a balky mule, it sank to the earth and cowered there, despite the frantic efforts of the surviving Jarmuthians to stir it to obedience.

By the strong amber light of the sun flare Nelson had a vision of the last two warriors swinging in apelike agility to the ground. They were giants, those two men of Jarmuth, and their conical helmets added additional stature. One of them, shouting an unintelligible taunt, reached for his belt to snatch out a fungus bomb, but Nelson, dropping on one knee, sent a bullet crashing between the Jarmuthian's scowling eyes. Even as he fell, the last of the six champions unwisely ignored his retortii and frantically sprang forward, razor-edged sword upraised.

Nelson frantically worked the ejector lever but only an empty click resulted! His heart sank. "Hell! the magazine's empty!"

HE had just time to swing the Winchester about and grasp its barrel as the Jarmuthian, with a loud shout, sprang in, slashing viciously at Nelson's unprotected neck. Using the clubbed rifle like a baseball bat, the American struck out with the strength of despair. There came a resonant clang as blade and barrel encountered each other. Steel is ever stronger than bronze, so Nelson had the satisfaction of seeing the Jarmuthian's sword blade break squarely in two near the hilt.

Horrified, the black bearded warrior glanced at the empty hilt in his hand but, courageous to the end, sprang in like a tiger to grapple with that small, agile man in khaki and serge.

"You would—eh?" gasped Nelson.

Putting all his strength behind a blow he whirled up the heavy Winchester, struck out and felt the solid walnut stock smash fair and square on the conical helmet. Like an eggshell the bronze helm broke and the six-pointed star above went spinning off into the dust. As a tree sways before it falls beneath a forester's ax, so the dark Jarmuthian giant tottered, while the wide dusty plain of Poseidon echoed with a rumbling, incredulous shout.

"There," choked Nelson, incredulous to be still alive, "I guess that'll be about all for to-day."

But he was wrong. From the ranks of Jarmuth rose a terrible, ominous cry and at the same time there broke out the sibilant hiss of a thousand retortii. From the Atlantean army came an answering yell and Nelson turned to race back to the shelter of Altorius' body-guard, pausing but to arouse the terrified hostages. Swiftly he cast loose their bonds and pointed to the nearest detachment of Atlanteans. Sobbing with joy the six girls fled for dear life just as the first of the allosauri went racing over the plains. Screaming, all-powerful and uncanny war dogs, they bounded grotesquely high in the air, plunging straight towards the Jarmuthian ranks which greeted them with a searing, billowing blast of their retortii. Though dozens of the terrible creatures fell kicking and writhing beneath the scalding discharge of the retortii, the main body, perhaps forty or fifty in number, sprang like rending fiends into the dense packed masses of Jarmuthian infantry.

OF the ensuing battle, Nelson had but the most confused recollections. The dominating impression was that the fray was awesome, horrible beyond power of description. He recalled feeding the five remaining cartridges into the magazine, then clapping on an

Atlantean noble's helmet. With Hero John at his side he joined in an furious headlong charge of the podoko corps.

Like a vast glittering wedge the gallant Atlantean lancers advanced steadily under shelter of the blue maxima vapor which, discharged by the protectons or light infantry, dispelled the scalding steam clouds launched from the Jarmuthian portable retortii.

"Halor vàn!" Hero John shouted the Atlantean war cry. "Halor vàn! Come Friend Nelson, this day shall the treacherous swine of Jarmuth drown in their own blood! Halor vàn!"

Nelson replied nothing. He was too busy drawing a bead on a gorgeously arrayed enemy officer who appeared to be directing the defence.

Faster and faster rushed the podokos, forty, fifty miles an hour, a carnate thunderbolt hurled straight at the enemy center. Under a hot fire of grenades dozens of the lancers fell and once, when a fungus bomb broke near by, Nelson saw half a dozen Atlanteans tumble from their saddles, the hideous yellow growths already sprouting from nostrils, mouth and ears. The turmoil became deafening, indescribable—like the roar of a crowded subway.

The American had a brief glimpse of a mountainous diplodocus assailed by half a dozen hissing, shrieking allosauri who, employing jaws and claws, ripped great, shuddering chucks of flesh from the agonized and unwieldy monster on whose back the frantic Jarmuthians fought with terrible ferocity.

AS agile as grasshoppers, those fierce war dogs ripped and worried their prey. One of them clung like a bulldog to the doomed diplodocus' head, though the twenty-foot neck writhed and whirled frantically in effort to shake it loose. Another allosaurus, whining with eagerness, actually clambered up the back of an assailed giant only to fall back under the blast of a retortii mounted in the howdah. Bathed in live steam, with bones showing through its melting, quivering flesh, the allosaurus collapsed backwards, but another instantly took its place and, gaining its goal with a terrific leap, made a shambles of the howdah, tearing the men in it apart as a lion does an antelope.

Nelson found himself very busy. The charging podokesos were now in the midst of the Jarmuthian heavy infantry, slashing down at a maze of yelling, black-bearded, Semitic faces. Once Nelson was nearly speared, shooting his assailant just as the lance glimmered over his heart. Again he saw the Atlantean hoplites beaten back amid a pestilential fog of fungus gas which stretched them in kicking, loathsome heaps on the dusty plain. The uproar became terrific, indescribable, as the whistling screams of the allosauri and the saurean bellows of the diplodoci rose above the shouts of the soldiery to fill the dust-laden air with a dreadful clamor. The battle now swayed critically; a feather's weight on either side and one army would roll back in red, irretrievable ruin. It was the psychological instant. Nelson sensed it unerringly.

"Look!" shouted Hero John, dashing a rivulet of blood from his eyes, "there fights the dog-begotten

Jereboam himself! Halor vàn! Smite, ye soldiers of Atlans! Smite!"

Following the line of the outstretched hand. Nelson caught a glimpse of an enormous, eagle nosed warrior who, clad in gleaming, diamond studded harness, fought like a paladin of old. Powerful as a dark Ares the sable browed Jereboam raged among the dismayed Atlantean hoplites, beating them to earth with terrible ferocity.

IT WAS a long shot, one he might readily have been forgiven in missing but with the speed of thought Victor Nelson sprang from his podoko, dropped on one knee behind a pile of corpses and, uttering a fervent prayer, fired full at Jereboam's black head.

The nearest combatants drew back momentarily at the unfamiliar thunder of the report and fell silent while the groans and shrieks of the wounded rose loud. As a man looking through many thickness of glass, so Nelson saw Jereboam reel on his splendidly caparisoned podoko, clasp both hands to his forehead and sink to earth.

Hero Giles, somewhere far in the Atlantean van, saw what transpired and capitalized it with the inspiration of a genius.

"Jereboam is dead!" he shouted in ringing tones, and flashed his red stained sword. "Woe to Jarmuth this day! Smite, ye sons of Atlans. Woe to Jarmuth—Jereboam is fallen!"

And smite hard the reinforced Atlanteans did. Filled with a new courage they advanced so determinedly that the disconcerted and dismayed Jarmuthians broke and fled in a disastrous, panic-stricken rout back over the plain of Poseidon towards the boiling river.

The ground was already carpeted with dead and with abandoned equipment, when fresh packs of allosauri were loosed on the fleeing Jarmuthians to wreak havoc indescribable and, ere long, only the triumphant, panting Atlanteans remained on the field.

CHAPTER SIX

THERE was music and high revelry in the fortress of Cierum that night, and Victor Nelson, embarrassed and flushed with the extravagant adoration of all Atlans, sat by the Emperor Altorius' side waiting, watching for the appearance of a humbled Jarmuthian delegation.

"Never since the world began has there been such a hero in Atlans!" cried Altorius, his face more Roman than ever. "Prithee tarry amongst us, Hero Nelson. Thou shalt be as my brother. A marble palace shalt thou have and twenty wives, each fair as those damsels which thou hast, by thy might, rescued from the profane altar of the fiend, Beelzebub!"

"Thanks," laughed Nelson heartily, and drained a large goblet of tawny wine. "I'd be delighted to stay, but the point is—He broke off short, for there came a sudden tramp of feet at the door of the great hall and there, just visible above the green crests of the royal guards, he recognized that pale, drawn face which had haunted him ever since he had returned to find the abandoned aeroplane.

"Dick!" he shouted. "Dick Alden!"

"Nelson!"

With that same irresistible form which had won a certain November classic for Harvard, Richard Alden bucked and plunged through a double rank of startled guards and came running across the marble floor, his eyes lit with an unspeakable gladness.

"Nelson! Nelson!" he panted. "What in hell are you doing up there?"

"Oh!" replied the aviator with an obvious joyous grin, "just visiting with my good friend, the Emperor."

ALDEN halted, on his handsome features a curious mixture of surprise and delight. "The Emperor?" he stammered. "You sitting beside an Emperor?"

"Would it not seem so?" inquired Altorius with a low laugh.

"It would," chuckled Alden. "Victor Nelson, as I remember, always was a good politician."

"And," thought Nelson, "I'll have to be a damn sight better one to get us out of Atlans without injuring Altorius' feelings. I don't suppose he'll ever be able to realize that all the desirable things in the world don't lie in this valley."

Throngs of brilliantly armored and plumed officers and courtiers, some of them nursing wounds and bandaged heads, came up to hail the mighty wanderer who had subdued the might of Jarmuth.

Flushed and pleased, as is any normal man under well-earned praise, Nelson shook one wiry fist after another, while Alden chatted with the Emperor. Nobles, officers and courtiers all pressed close to fawn upon the new hero—but, far back in the council chamber, a group of dark robed priests were crowded together. Haranguing the priests was a fierce, white bearded old man who seemed to be arguing violently.

"Hum!" thought the American. "That's at least one outfit that doesn't like the way I part my hair. Wonder what devilment the priests are cooking up?"

HE was not long in finding out, for the black robed arch-priest suddenly left his group of underlings to boldly make his way forward, while princes, courtiers and warriors drew respectfully aside and bent their heads.

"Hail! All conquering Emperor!" The stern old man halted squarely before Altorius' gem encrusted throne, while Alden checked some remark to look curiously down upon the hawk-featured arch-priest.

Altorius flushed and the lines about his mouth tightened, from which Nelson guessed that there was more than a little bad blood between the spiritual and temporal heads of the empire.

"What wouldst thou, oh Heracles?"

"I would know why the all powerful Wanderer, of whom thou makest so much, did not rescue Princess Altara?"

The Emperor stiffened. "Her rescue, being impossible of accomplishment, was not nominated in the agreement," he said coldly. "The Wanderer has in full carried out his share—and so shall we. Honored and beloved of Atlans, these great warriors shall abide among us in peace."

Here Nelson thought it wise to dispel any illusions Altorius might entertain about their staying in Atlans. "No, oh Splendor: remember, our agreement was that, should I conquer the Jarmuthian champions, Alden and I were to be allowed to go free."

"Nay, oh Splendor," fiercely broke in the arch-priest, "permit them not to go. I tell thee the Princess Altara *must* be restored to Atlans! Else…" A distinct note of threat crept into the old man's voice. "…else evil days shall fall upon this empire, and the line of Hudson will wither and fade."

Up sprang Altorius in a towering rage. "Sirrah! Dost dare make threats to thy liege lord?"

FIRE flashed from the young Emperor's bright blue eyes, and under their fierce glare the old man quailed and stepped back with eyes lowered.

"Altorius keeps his word," the Emperor thundered. "The strangers shall go, though all the black-robed kites in the realm say me nay. The word of a Hudsonian prince is as sure as the fire of Pelion. Get thee gone, rash priest!"

A long moment, the two strangely contrasting figures glared hard at each other, the young, splendid Emperor and the malevolent, withered old man.

"The Gods demand their daughter," cried Heracles in parting, "and woe to him who says them nay!"

With this parting shot, the arch-priest turned and, scarlet faced, stalked from the council room, while Altorius threw back his head and roared with laughter.

"Come, oh ye Heroes, ye princes and captains! Come, let us make festival before these mighty wanderers go their way!"

Roar upon roar of enthusiasm echoed through the marble throne room, and Nelson would have felt wholly at ease had not that little knot of priests remained gathered like ill-omened carrion crows about the door.

Muttering among themselves, they were watching him with a curious intentness that aroused deep misgivings in the American's mind, and it was with something like a sigh that he joined the procession forming to proceed to the triumphal feast on which the wealth and luxury of the whole empire of Atlans had been lavished.

CHAPTER SEVEN

THATS one of the fixed retortiis I was speaking about," remarked Victor Nelson as he paused to point out a tapering brass tube which was mounted on a platform above the long staircase up which he and Alden were toiling. "It's a big brute: see how small the gunners look beside it? These steam guns are wonderful things."

The younger aviator sighed. "I've had enough of miracles," he said wiping his flushed features and hitching a small pack higher on his leather-clad shoulders. "All I want to do is to lay my weary eyes on the plane again. What with these ghastly allosauri, diplodocuses and other monsters, I'm damn well fed up with this place."

Nelson settled his Winchester rifle more comfortably into the hollow of his arm. "Correct. So am I. But we can't say Altorius didn't do right by our Nell. Good Lord, what a triumph he gave us!" The dark pilot's smile flashed from beneath his neat, close-clipped black mustache. "Wait till Cartier gets a peep at those diamonds he gave us."

Panting, the two halted by mutual consent. "Ever see so many stairs?" grunted Nelson. "Three more flights and we'll be into the tunnel; ah, there's the opening. I only hope these blighters haven't hurt the plane."

Before resuming the climb Nelson shifted his rifle, idly regarding the armored gunners just above him; then suddenly he stiffened his wiry body with a loud, sharp cry. "Look out, Dick! What the devil? Those damn fools ahead are swinging the retortii across our—"

THE DARK haired aviator's words were drowned out in a deafening, hissing roar that burst from the great retortii's throat, and his heart gave a great convulsive leap at the sight. Was this an accident—or treachery? An accident of course. Somehow he could not bring himself to think that Altorius would break his pledged word. Projected in a shimmering white arm the scalding death vapor shot across the staircase, its hot breath licking the faces of the startled and angry Americans, and quickly forcing them to turn and run downwards to avoid being scalded.

"Now what in the devil are these idiots trying to do?" gasped Nelson, anxiously eyeing the red-crested warriors who, peering down through the blue lenses of their helmets, watched the khaki-clad aviators but made no effort to realign their retortii. "Hero Giles'll skin those fools alive if he ever hears of this. Guess we'd better wait a minute: they'll soon shut off the steam."

Shielding his face from the steam clouds that obliterated all view of the staircase above, Alden stood watching the billowing steam clouds in silent awe.

"Terrible, aren't they, Vic?" he remarked. "I've never seen those big fellows in action. They make the portable variety look like water pistols."

*Yes, there came a strange,
but welcome sight.*

PHALANXES OF ATLANS
By F. V. W. Mason

AS the steam barrier showed no signs of abating, an uneasy gleam crept into Nelson's dark eye, and with jaw grimly set, he cocked the Winchester and turned with the intention of lodging a complaint at the next station below; but, to his utter dismay, he beheld bronze armored figures on the next platform now training their long-muzzled steam gun across the stair. Even as he sprang back, the deadly white vapor hissed forth from the second retortii, completely barring further retreat down the stair. Like an icy flood the chill of impending doom invaded Nelson's soul. This was no accidental discharge, for with the slightest change of direction in the deflection of either retortii, death would descend upon him and his companion.

Swiftly speech became impossible, as the roar of the huge retortii was deafening; the two were lost in the heart of an opaque cloud which completely blotted out the copper-hued Atlantean sky. Hot blood surged into Nelson's head while he became aware of ghostly and stealthy figures advancing through the shimmering billows of vapor. Up, up, they came, like dream men, their eyes weird and unreal. Cursing the treachery of their late host, Nelson and Alden watched dozens upon dozens of hoplites come swarming up the stairs in solid, dully-gleaming ranks. Apparently intent to take them prisoners, the foremost Atlanteans made a rush, giving the American time to fire just twice.

Unable to retreat, the helpless aviators stood to meet the engulfing wave of hoplites. Nelson struck out as hard as he could at those yelling, red-bearded faces, though he knew the effort was hopeless. He was dimly conscious that Alden, not far away, also fought with the vigor of despair.

With a sense of savage satisfaction, the dark haired aviator felt his fist impact solidly into a yelling, sweating face; then something struck his head and, amid a miniature sunburst, his senseless form sank limply on the damp stones of the great staircase.

AFTER AN interval, the length of which he did not know, Victor Nelson opened his eyes slowly, for his head throbbed like a savage's war drum. Uttering a stifled groan he shut the lids to still an overpowering sense of nausea which gripped him, but a moment later he made another attempt to discover in what sort of place he found himself. Gradually, his eyes became accustomed to a curious orange-red glare beyond a series of bars. Bars? The idea fixed itself in his benumbed brain; bars meant prison! Yes, those grim blank walls bore out the assumption. He lay on the damp stone floor of what must be a fairly spacious cell. Beneath his leather aviator's jacket he shuddered. "Jail, eh? What a nice place to wake up in!"

A groan from behind him prompted Nelson to painfully raise his head and look about. He blinked dazedly, meanwhile trying to focus his eyes, then he heaved a faint sigh of relief as his gaze encountered the muscular, well-proportioned figure of Richard Alden, who half sat, half reclined, against one of the grey stone walls, burying a ghastly pale face between trembling hands.

"You hurt?" To speak, Nelson drew a slightly deeper breath and at once became conscious of a horrible, throat-wrenching stench. Dimly, he recalled having once before encountered such an odor; when was it? Oh, yes; during the Great War when he'd stumbled into a dugout tenanted by long unburied corpses. A cold finger stabbed at his brain. Corpses.

"Are you hurt, Dick?" he repeated hoarsely.

THE lax figure stirred and Alden's blonde head was raised slowly. "I don't know." His voice came very thickly. "I—I'm still dizzy. What's happened?"

"Damned if I know; but those bright boys have evidently heaved us into a calaboose of some kind!"

Nelson, on peering about, had discovered that one end of the cell was closed only by a series of massive bronze bars; the two other walls were solid masonry; while the fourth was also solid but fitted with a small oval door of bronze.

"Calaboose? The hell you say!" Alden coughed feebly. "My God, but that steam was terrible stuff. I nearly smothered before I got knocked out."

Slowly, the younger aviator looked about, and suddenly his eyes widened in an expression of indescribable horror.

"Look!" Alden's voice had died to a shaken whisper. "My God, Nelson, we're finished! Look at that allosaurus!"

FOLLOWING the line indicated by the pilot's shaking forefinger, Nelson peered out through the series of great bars while a shudder shook his aching body. Though he had seen these fearful monsters on many occasions, yet it was never from such a position as that in which he now found himself. To his ears came a sibilant hissing like that of a thousand serpents; and, quivering in every nerve, he forced his eyes open once again, to discover that the cell which he and his companion occupied was but one of a series of cells surrounding a huge square in which were imprisoned perhaps twenty or thirty of those horrible, gargoylesque creatures which were the Atlantean dogs of war. Some thirty-four feet in length, the enormous, slate-grey monsters hopped leisurely about, their warty hides and huge luminous eyes betraying their reptilian origin. In shape the allosauri resembled loathsome and titanic kangaroos as they lumbered awkwardly to and fro, picking viciously at what appeared to be fragments of human flesh and bones.

While the two prisoners crouched paralyzed with horror, one of the nightmarish creatures came hopping over and, pressing a head as big as a steam scoop against the bars, stared in with huge, pale green eyes. A long minute the ghastly creature remained looking in, clearly outlined by the orange glow from outside.

THE doomed aviators found something fearfully fascinating about those narrow vertical irises set in pupils the size of dinner plates. Uttering a deep growl, the allosaurus shuffled nearer, and impatiently rubbed its huge, bullet head against the bars; then gripped the ponderous bronze bars with its ridiculously small front legs to shake the whole grille-work with a savagery that dislocated bits of plaster and made the metal reverberate. While Nelson and Alden shrank flat against the far wall, a scarlet tongue at least four feet long flicked the air but a few feet from their bloodless, sweating visages. Becoming irritated at the sturdiness of the barrier, the mountainous reptile tugged harder and hissed, filling the cell with a foul exhalation that stank like the reeks of smoldering rags.

Nelson's wavering consciousness reeled, and a mad, dreadful fear, like that a dreamer suffers in the grip of nightmare, invaded his being. He felt the hairs rising on the nape of his neck.

But, with a squall of rage, the monster abandoned its futile efforts and leaped away. Feigning indifference, the allosaurus picked up a half-gnawed skull with its tiny forelegs; and, while the prisoners watched, it stuffed the head into a maw twice the size of an elephant's and crunched the gruesome tidbit as easily as a boy would a walnut. Presently it shuffled off to rejoin the hideous herd in the center of the court.

"Nice kind of a jail we've been thrown into. Wish I could understand what's happened." Alden buried his face in his hands. "It kind of looks as though Altorius had a change of heart."

NELSON replied nothing, but sat staring fixedly out into the horrible court.

"Somehow, I don't think Altorius would do such a thing," he said at last. "Let's think back and see if we can't piece this treachery together."

"Wish I had your faith in the Emperor—but I haven't." Alden's handsome face twisted itself into a wry smile.

"Let's see, now," persisted Nelson, fingering a square jaw upon which sprouted a thick growth of reddish bristles. "There was a deputation of priests to see Altorius yesterday. They were clamoring for the return of Altara—the Sacred Virgin—and looked pretty mad when he put them off."

"Maybe this is the private doing of the priests," admitted Alden. "Anyway, we're in one devil of a fix. There's certainly no way out of this calaboose—and those damned brutes out there look hungry."

Nelson frowned, deep in thought. "Wish I could find a reasonable explanation. I really don't think it's Altorius; still, that's what you get for mixing in on the politics of these forgotten kingdoms."

"But," reminded the other, "you had no choice, old lad. Remember, you mixed in to save me."

From across the courtyard rang a loud, penetrating shriek of fear that made the two aviators spring to their feet and rush to the bars. Peering across the court, they discovered three naked men shrieking and clinging frantically to the bars of an exactly similar cell.

"What's wrong with them?" demanded Alden as the agonized screams rang louder still.

"I don't know," was Alden's breathless reply. "But what's that noise?"

A curious metallic clanking sound filled the poisoned air, and for a moment Nelson remained utterly puzzled. Then, as the noise grew louder, the allosauri commenced to betray a strange restlessness. They ceased basking and feeding, and their hideous heads commenced to dart quickly this way and that.

WHILE the terrific shrieks of the wretches across the court rang to the copper-hued sky, the two Americans remained in doubt; then all at once the chill of death gripped their hearts, as they saw the bars of that cell directly opposite slowly but surely rising! Uttering heart-rending cries, the doomed prisoners clung frantically to stay the vanishing barrier separating them from those appalling man-eaters. But, disdainful of their pitiful efforts, the bronze bars rose relentlessly with metallic rattlings and janglings from some unseen mechanism.

Rooted to the floor, both Americans watched the distant grille vanish into the upper stone-work and heard the ghastly hissing as the allosauri herd commenced to move forward. Sick and shaken, Nelson beheld one of the doomed men cling in desperation to the bars; he was lifted clear of the floor and borne towards the ceiling, meanwhile venting his terror with such screams as could otherwise have risen only from an inquisitor's torture chamber.

The tragedy was swiftly completed. Half a dozen of the nearest allosauri, taller than any giraffes, suddenly sprang forward, their long, naked tails rising as their gait increased. Snarling horribly, the vast slate-colored beasts plunged into the cell, terminating shrieks of mortal terror. Backs broader than bus tops squirmed and tugged, then one of the loathsome monsters reappeared carrying in its dripping jaws a mangled, yet struggling victim much as a cat carries a mouse. In a trice the other allosauri came rushing eagerly up, seeking to snatch the prey from the first monster.

Nelson stiffened. "Great God! And that's what'll happen to us!"

WEAKENED by his head wound, and blind with nausea, he stumbled to the rear of the cell to collapse upon a pile of foul straw, littered with equipment which the superstitious captors must have condemned together with the owners.

Nelson sank upon them, then stiffened, for his outflung hand had encountered a hard, familiar outline. It was a .45 automatic pistol.

A moment's furious search revealed that the captors had missed or not understood the use of the weapon in Alden's leather flying coat.

"God, but we're lucky," Nelson panted. "The Atlanteans never saw this pistol of yours. They're only used to my rifle."

Hope lit Alden's features, then faded. "But what good is a .45 against brutes like those? Might at well have a pop gun!"

"Still we're lucky," grunted Nelson, delighted to find the magazine yet filled. "Can't tell what's ahead. Yes, we're the luckiest—"

He broke off in quick alarm. From overhead had come a premonitory clang! Somewhere a tackle whined and, with a sense of suffocation, both men realised that now the bars of *their* prison were beginning to creep up into a long slit in the stone ceiling!

Cold fingers of fear clutched Nelson's heart as the terrible allosauri, their jaws yet dripping redly, wheeled about at the familiar sound—to stand listening. Up and up crept the ponderous grille, while the allosauri commenced to shuffle forward, fixing on their next victims enormous, unblinking green eyes.

WHILE the whole loathsome cell spun about, Victor Nelson forced stiff fingers to throw off the safety catch as the nearest allosaurus opened its cavernous mouth in anticipation, displaying an array of wicked, curved teeth, as long and sharp as steel bayonets. Standing some fifteen feet high or more at the shoulder the horrible creature's body was; it all but blotted out the light. The bars rose inexorably. Now they were waist high... Now above Nelson's head... In a moment would come the rush.

Richard Alden stood up straight and squared his shoulders. "Good-by, Vic," he said, in clear, unafraid tones. "I don't imagine that .45 will even tickle those ghastly brutes."

Nelson nodded. "All over but the cheering," he replied with that strange, macabre humor which often comes to solace men about to die.

"See you in church." There was an equally gallant lightness to Alden's reply.

The dark haired pilot, with a curious, detached sense of unreality, stepped into the middle of the room, the automatic in his hand seeming no more potent than a water pistol, for a ponderous, lambent eyed monster was now hopping forward. While minute particles of dust and dirt rained down from the disappearing barrier, the foremost allosaurus opened its enormous jaws, uttered an eery scream and charged straight at the unbarred cell.

Drawing a deep breath, Nelson raised the .45, sighted, and, remembering his former experience, fired at the enormous right eye. As in a dream, he felt the recoil. The monster neither slowed nor swerved in the least, though its great, saucer-like eye disintegrated horribly. Immediately Nelson swiftly sighted at the other eye and fired, just as the allosaurus' shadow filled the threshold.

Crack! A swirl of bitter smoke stung the aviator's staring eyes. He'd hit; he knew it!

CYCLOPEAN moments followed as the blinded monster dashed forward, missed the circular door, and, butting his head against the stone wall to the left, fell completely stunned, effectively blocking the doorway with its huge body. One enormous hind leg, fully ten feet long, and equipped with three razor-like claws, projected into the cell and lashed aimlessly back and forth, forcing the two prisoners to dodge wildly.

There ensued that indescribable kind of a moment when men go mad. Outside the cell the ravenous herd pounced upon their fallen mate and with hideous grunts and snarls promptly commenced to tear it apart. The shaken prisoners realized that the rending jaws would before long undoubtedly remove the temporary obstacle; but meanwhile the hideous hissing and the fetid stench of the allosauri breath made the cell a mad-house.

Gradually, the gigantic carcass at the door commenced to quiver and roll violently under the ferocious tugs of the eager feasters. A gap of light appeared over the huge haunches, and, all at once, another of those terrible heads slipped over the carcass and into the cell.

Again the .45 thundered, lighting the darkened cell with a brief orange flame. A noise like the furious trumpeting of a dozen elephants nearly blew Nelson flat as the wounded monster drew back its head, but the respite promised to be short, for the other reptiles only re-doubled their horrid, cannibalistic rending of the carcass. When the barrier was removed there would be a general rush which the shaken aviators could not hope to stay.

SUDDENLY, Alden uttered a low shout and pointed to the small, oval door which had, up to this point, remained securely bolted and shut. It was swinging gradually open, rimmed with a strong reddish light.

Wide-eyed, and with black hair streaming lank over his forehead, Nelson, in the act of reloading, swung about to meet this new menace. Hell! What point was there in prolonging the pitiful struggle? What was happening?

Slowly, the door swung back, and a rosy glow lit the opening, a glow that became as strong as the gleam of a spotlight. Then, slowly, a glittering, green-crested helmet of highly polished bronze appeared, and, under it, Hero Giles' familiar features, now distorted by a terrible fear. The blue eyes seemed enormous. "Quickly!" he called. "Quick or ye are lost!"

Unbelieving of the reprieve, both the aviators stared an instant at that martial figure clad in brazen armor liberally studded with enormous diamonds and emeralds, then leaped forward with the speed of desperation, for from behind came a fierce squalling from the allosauri. As he darted towards the door Nelson had a glimpse of the carcass blocking the door commencing to slip sidewise.

Alden was already out and Nelson sped through the door barely in time to escape the razor-sharp talons of the foremost allosaurus as it scrambled into the deserted cell with a resounding bellow of disappointed fury.

CHAPTER EIGHT

AS the door clanged shut, drowning out the allosauri's furious screams, both aviators, shaken to the depths of their beings, could do nothing but stare about them in surprise. Completely surrounding and protecting the exit stood a double rank of hoplites in bronze armor. Like unreal automata, they remained utterly motionless, fixed in the various postures of an ancient Macedonian phalanx, their broad backs gleaming dully in the light of the neon flares. As in a dream, Nelson recognized on top of each spearsman's casque the graceful Atlantean military crest—a metal dolphin from the back of which sprouted a series of bright blue feathers, arranged like a dorsal fin.

"Thank Poseidon, ye still live!" cried Hero Giles, gripping their hands eagerly. "I had fear for ye, oh my friends."

Nelson grinned. "You cut the rescue act pretty fine, but of course we're damned grateful. And now..." Eagerly seizing the Hero's splendidly muscled arm. "...in God's name tell us what's happened. Why we were arrested and—nearly made into allosaurus fodder?"

Hero Giles turned from snapping an order to a subaltern who was peering down a great, shadowy hallway with a distinctly uneasy manner.

"Much," he said. "Scarcely had ye two departed from Heliopolis than the priests, mad with rage over Altara's continued captivity, dared to seize the person of His Splendor and proclaim a regency. Herakles, the arch-priest is—"

FROM far down the gloomy, vaulted corridor came a faint sound, rather like the cheering of a crowd in the distance. The hoplites, standing about, turned their helmeted heads and stared uneasily, their brazen armor glowing dully with each movement.

"I'll tell ye more later, but now..." Hero Giles' voice took on a ringing quality like the clash of steel. "...there is work to be done. To rescue ye, oh Hero Nelson, I slew the guards at the lower gate, for this prison lies in the hands of a caitiff rogue, Hero Edmund, one who clings to the priestly party. We had best be off lest we be trapped and slaughtered like rats in a pit."

Very distinctly to the ears of the aviator now came the dull clash of equipment and the tread of feet.

"Forward! We must hasten to reach the podokos waiting below," cried Hero Giles, settling his ponderous helmet more squarely on his leonine head.

At once the escort of fifteen-odd hoplites commenced to move down the corridor to the left, their hands tightly gripping the butts of their retortii pistols. At their head ran Hero Giles, and by his side Alden and Victor Nelson, who gripped his .45 vowing never again to return to that ghastly cell.

A long ringing cry from the rear brought home the dread realization that the enemy had appeared. Looking back, Nelson could see the far end of the great corridor filled with menacing figures. Then his heart leaped like a deer in a thicket, for *from ahead* sounded the clash of weapons! The rescue party's retreat was cut off!

HERO Giles acted with the speed of a veteran accustomed to emergencies. "Forward!" he roared, making the bare walls reverberate and rumble with his voice. *"Halor vàn! Ula Storr!"* (make ready for your retortii)

As by magic, there appeared before the retreating force a double rank of blue-crested hoplites who debouched from a side passage into the hall and clawed desperately for fungus bombs and retortii. Evidently they had not expected to come upon the invaders so abruptly.

"Storr!" Like a brazen trumpet's call, the voice of Hero Giles rang out the order to fire—which was instantly drowned out in the furious hissing of the retortii of his followers.

Ever watchful, Nelson fired at a gigantic officer who, avoiding the first steam jets, flung back his arms to hurl one of the deadly fungus bombs among the rescuers. Shattering the bronze helmet, the American's bullet struck the Atlantean squarely between the eyes, but nevertheless the stricken officer's grenade rolled forward and burst among the hindermost of Hero Giles' followers. Instantly, the deadly green mold flung itself upon the nearest hoplites and in a moment they crashed to the smooth granite floor, the yellowish growths already sprouting from nose, mouth and ears.

In the corridor reigned chaos, for Hero Giles' followers were now turning the full fury of their retortii upon the rank of men barring further flight. With dreadful ease, the scalding steam struck dead the opposing warriors, stripping the flesh from their bones as easily as a boy peels a banana.

Amid the swirling white clouds, Nelson had ghastly visions of yellow skulls, of steaming accoutrement, of limp heaps of disintegrating bodies; then silence fell, and, before he quite realized it, he, together with Alden and three hoplites who had survived the disastrous fungus grenade, were bounding along after Hero Giles' glittering figure as he led the way down one passage after another.

LOUDER than ever rang the fierce cry from the rear. Behind him Nelson could see dozens upon dozens of yelling pursuers, and knew that if he were to live he must run as never before.

Into a succession of spacious rooms dashed the fugitives; on through deserted armories where hundreds of bronze helmets dangled in orderly rows; and across silent barrack halls.

Closer and closer sounded the pursuing feet, spurring the runners to an even more headlong gait.

All at once a door loomed to the right; into this darted Hero Giles and after him pounded the two Americans and three hoplites. In an instant the six men set their shoulder to the ponderous bronze door and swung it to, just as the hiss of a retortii on the other side rose above the mad, blood-hungry clamor of the momentarily baffled rebels. Gasping and sweat-bathed, the fugitives paused only an instant.

"We've gained a short passage," gasped the Atlantean wrenching off his helmet and breast plate. The veins stood out in great blue cords on his forehead, for the weight of the armor could not have been inconsiderable. "Below wait our podokos."

Nelson stripped off his leather coat, following the example of the hoplites, who swiftly divested themselves of such cumbersome equipment as could readily be removed. Then, while the shouts of the thwarted pursuers swelled like a demonic chorus, and while feathers of steam crept under the great door, Hero Giles spun about and, with his short yellow hair gleaming bright, led on down another series of passages.

ALL at once the fugitives, now reduced by exhaustion to five, found themselves on a balcony overlooking the great valley of Atlans. Before them opened an enormous staircase and down this they dashed at top speed, infinitely relieved to be once more in the open air.

Running like hunted stags, the fugitives had descended but a third of the great staircase, when, from behind, came a sudden, menacing cry that warned Nelson that the pursuers had, after going a longer way around, come once more in sight.

"Ah! Poseidon blast the traitorous Edmund and his varlets! See?" panted Hero Giles pointing to a huge arch from beneath which was issuing a glittering column of shouting, swift running warriors at whose head dashed a splendidly-proportioned figure that must be Hero Edmund.

With the speed of the hunted, Hero Giles bounded forward, taking three and four steps at a stride, his jade green cloak snapping out behind. Down, ever downwards over the endless flight of stairs the aviators followed him until, spent and panting, the hard pressed five plunged down a final circular staircase and so gained a courtyard where waited a detachment of armored lancers whose yellow plumes and pennons shone bright in the glare of the flame suns. Staring anxiously upwards, the troopers nevertheless stood to attention in an orderly rank beside those curious Atlantean mounts called podokos.

During all his sojourn in Atlans, Nelson had never become used to the hideous and awe-inspiring podokos which closely resembled the allosauri but were only eighteen feet long. Like the other monsters, they had tremendously developed hind legs which promised the speed now so vital for escape and safety. Ready in the tooth-studded jaws of each podoko was fitted a bronze bit together with a bridle and reins; and cinched up on each creature's back was one of those curious Atlantean saddles, which was built up at the cantle to overcome the downward slope of the podokos' spines.

Need for vital haste was but too obvious and, as he drew near, Hero Giles gasped the command to be off.

"Quick," he shouted, his scarred visage flushed and sweat-bathed. "Saddles! Speed! Speed! Cling fast as your beasts arise!"

ALL five literally hurled themselves into gorgeously caparisoned saddles. Instantly, the urging squatting podokos leaped to their feet.

It was the work of a moment for Nelson to wrench his reptile around, for already Alden and the Atlantean cavalrymen were speeding across the wide paved court, their lance pennons fluttering bravely in the orange-hued glare.

At top speed the rescuers dashed for a great, oval gateway while the podokos increased their gait; like aeroplanes gathering speed, the faster the weird creatures traveled, the higher arose their tails.

Then, following the frightened, backward glances of the hard-riding, red-haired lancers, Nelson suddenly discovered a new and terrible cause for this headlong flight, for, issuing from an unbarred gateway, came perhaps a dozen of *the terrible and enormous allosauri*, which, spying the fleeing cavalry, instantly gave chase.

With a sense of despair, the aviators heard the ferocious bellows booming from behind and watched the appallingly swift progress of those uncouth monsters as, leaping high into the air, the allosauri covered between fifty and sixty feet at a single bound.

"They'll get you," cried an inner voice in Nelson's being. "They'll catch you sure." But the small and lithe podokos, sensing death leaping up from the rear, stretched out their slender, snake-like heads, stood on tiptoe, and, pressing their small forelegs tight against their chests, commenced to run far faster than any horse could gallop. Nevertheless, the allosauri came bounding up like colossal kangaroos, uttering weird, screaming roars that brought a chill of imminent death to the fugitives.

Casting a quick glance over his shoulder, Nelson's blood froze to find an allosaurus not more than seventy yards behind, and making terrible exertions to close that slender gap! Nearer and nearer coursed the incredible monster, body rocking in its terrific stride, dreadful jaws wide apart—jaws that could, without an effort, cut a horse in half.

A FEAR such as he had never known racked Nelson's consciousness as he found he was hindermost of the cavalcade, which was strung out like a field of racers. The other riders crouched low in their saddles like jockeys, lances held straight out before them, and furiously goaded their strange mounts with curious hooks. Nelson was vastly relieved to get a glimpse of Alden far in the lead, almost beside the Atlantean Prince. His podoko was evidently better than the average.

Faster and faster pursuers and pursued raced across level meadows, over straight, white roads and rolling grain fields. Wind whistled madly in Nelson's ears, filled his eyes with tears, and made his short, dark hair snap, but two huge allosauri were now not twenty yards behind and *gaining with appalling speed!*

On the verge of madness, Nelson hammered his heels into the podoko's scaly side and wished he dared let go the saddle horn to draw his pistol, but to loose his grip was to risk falling off.

Closer and closer! Two enormous nightmarish heads were actually snapping at the fleeing podoko's tail. Then fear must have inspired the reptile Nelson bestrode, for it put on a sudden desperate burst of speed which carried it past the next two lancers. In passing he glimpsed the doomed wretches, pale-faced and horrified, as they frantically goaded their failing podokos.

A moment later, piercing screams from somewhere not far behind assailed Nelson's ears, but when he looked to the rear once more it was to find that a wide gap had opened between him and the great monsters behind. Evidently, the heavy-built allosauri were unable to long maintain the terrific pace set by the smaller and more agile podokos whose maximum speed Nelson judged to be well over sixty miles an hour.

THE pilot's eyes narrowed on beholding, in clear relief and not far away, the majestic, whitish outline of mighty Heliopolis, whose lofty towers, graceful domes and frowning citadels shone pink under the leaping, blinding glare on Mount Pelion.

"Well we certainly picked a wonderful time to drop in on this God-forsaken country," grunted Alden as the walls of Heliopolis loomed ever nearer. "We seem to have crashed into some of the busiest days that they've had in centuries. How many shots you got?"

Nelson, swaying to the steady trot of his podoko, hesitated.

"Only five. An I'll be damned if I know what's happening next. I suppose it's all going to depend on Hero Giles. Looks as though the nobles were bent on restoring Altorius—if he's not dead by now."

Alden tugged powerfully at the strange bridle that controlled his beast. "The priests wouldn't dare kill him, but it surely looks like their rebellion has gained a lot of headway."

For the next several moments Alden's clear, blue eyes swept over the towering battlements, gorgeously-sculptured temples and curious stepped pyramids, which now loomed very near at hand and cast their rugged outlines sharp against the copper-colored heavens.

"Maybe there's some way we can work this revolution trouble to help us," suggested Nelson, without enthusiasm. "If we could play off one crowd against the other—"

His remarks were cut short as the foremost of the lancers slowed before the sight of an enormous bronze gate that was looming not far ahead. On the vast main panel was a beautifully-wrought dolphin curling about a trident—symbol of the imperial power now so sorely tried. Beyond that gate, breathlessly mused Nelson, lay Heliopolis and an unknown fate.

CHAPTER NINE

IT would have taken no trained eye to observe that something very unusual had happened in Atlans. Some of Heliopolis' many wide streets were quite deserted save for several small, bright-red cat-like reptiles that the Atlanteans sheltered as pets, but in other thoroughfares large throngs of people milled uneasily about, while listening to the impassioned harangue of black-robed priests. Everywhere business was at a standstill, shops were closed and markets tenantless.

Riding at an easy hopping gallop, the aviators urged their green, scaly mounts to the side of Hero Giles, for here and there some wandering citizens, spying the Americans, would yell shrill curses and shake their fists. Reining in, Nelson demanded to know the reason for this unaccountable hostility.

"'Tis the work of our gentle and holy priests," explained Hero Giles with a hard laugh. "They have told the populace ye are magicians seeking to set other gods above Poseidon."

"Nonsense," rapped the American, looking about uneasily. "We've never given two thin damns about anything except getting back to our plane."

"So I know," was the Atlantean's preoccupied reply; "but this spawn of Herakles' temples speak loud, and the loutish populace hearkens to their lies!"

"But what the devil is all this revolt about?" broke in Alden. "Why were we arrested? You started to tell us at the prison."

HERO Giles frowned as he pulled his podoko into a gracefully carved gateway of green marble. "There's but little to add, for 'tis all very simple. The priests have laid impious hands on His Splendor, Altorius, and imprisoned him in the great temple of Poseidon. We nobles have defied the arch-priest, for the dog-conceived Jereboam already marshals his forces for a fresh attack, knowing that Atlans is sore beset by internal strife. Have patience for now we go to the council chamber, where ye shall hear everything."

To say that the newcomers found the council of nobles in a furore would be to put it mildly. Their angry voices carried far down the beautifully ornamented corridors of the Imperial Palace, which was used as headquarters.

"Sounds like a dog-fight going on in there," muttered Alden anxiously. "Don't like the sound of it a bit. I hope they feel kindly towards us."

Nelson, swinging along with his ragged shirt fluttering like a scarecrow's, nodded. "Yes, so do I. But I guess they need our help or Hero Giles wouldn't have risked his life to save us."

Conscious of the value of appearances, the dark-haired aviator unconsciously straightened his frayed black tie, buttoned the sleeves of his khaki flannel shirt and otherwise made pathetic attempts at improving his appearance as the clamor of wrangling voices grew loud down the corridor.

His wide shoulders swinging to his stride, Hero Giles flung open a door, beautifully wrought with leaping podokos, and halted on the threshold.

"Death!" rumbled a voice from inside. "I say death to the Wanderers! Let us make our peace with the priests, lest they slay His Splendor forthwith."

"And that's what I call a nice friendly greeting," was Alden's murmured comment. "Better get your gat handy, Vic. I'll bet they've got a reception committee of retortii men behind the door."

THERE was no time for Nelson to reply because now the threshold was at hand. Inside, seated at a table, he had an impression of perhaps ten or fifteen scarred and angry-looking veteran nobles whose green cloaks and bejeweled armor revealed their high rank.

In mid-dispute they halted, eyeing the three figures in the doorway with curiously conflicting expressions. Some smiled a relieved welcome, some stared in surprise, but not a few greeted the Americans with lowering brows and angry, threatening eyes.

"Harken," Hero Giles greeted them. "By Poseidon's grace the Wanderers were saved from a vile death. Rise Heroes, and bid them welcome!"

"Ah, the Wanderers!" In an instant Hero John was wringing Nelson's hand. "Oh blessed hour! I had feared for ye both. Welcome, Hero Alden!"

A faint flush crept over the young man's wan and trouble-lined face. "'Tis well ye've come," he whispered. "The council was prepared to change their intent towards ye."

A grizzled, one-eyed prince arose, and leveling an accusing forefinger at Nelson shouted, "'Tis he hath caused the rebellion. Slay him!"

"Nay!" thundered the Hero Giles, "and forget not, Hero Paul—*I* am senior Prince of Atlans!"

ON the great white marble council chamber silence fell, while from wonderfully carved ivory and gold chairs the harassed, yellow-bearded princes regarded the two uneasy Americans.

"Hearken, Hero Giles!" rasped another dark-browed officer in a plain, much-dented red breast plate. "I side with Paul. Away with them, I say! Time is too precious. Do not the dark hordes of Jereboam beat back our frontiers?"

Hero Giles glowered and sat bolt upright in his chair—a strange disordered figure among his gorgeously robed and armored peers. "Thou wert ever a hothead! I prithee pause a moment! Remember how the dark-haired Wanderer once aided our imprisoned Emperor, whom Poseidon protect! Perchance, Hero Nelson and his friend once more can aid us in this, our hour of need."

A chorus of variously opined voices broke out, while Nelson with an eye to possible violence stood ready.

"Silence! Sirrah!" The fierce old veteran banged a powerful fist on a golden dolphin head forming his chair arm. "This idle wrangling accomplishes naught, and a thousand weighty matters await our attention. Is it true the phalanxes at Tricca have risen for the priests?"

BEFORE Hero Giles could reply, a stalwart guard at the door flung it open to admit a dust and sweat-bathed courier who, darting forward, flung himself at Hero Giles' no less dusty feet. While the yellow-haired Prince started back muttering in amazement, the runner raised a shaking hand.

"Woe, woe to Atlans!" he panted. "Jarmuthian retortii men have crossed the boiling river. Cierum is fallen! Its garrison is drenched in clouds of fungus gas. But a handful escaped!"

"Speak on: is that all?" A terribly intent expression crept over the aquiline faces around the council table.

"Nay, spare thy servant!" begged the green kilted courier, raising sweaty, imploring hands. "I—I dare not—"

"Speak!" snarled Hero Giles, his blue eyes terribly lit. "Speak!—else thy carcass shall be flung to the pteranodons."

Wild-eyed, the fellow blinked fearfully about. The grim-lipped nobles edged closer. Nelson, realizing all that lay at stake, watched intently, conscious that Alden was now by his side.

"I—I, Her Sacred Holiness, Altara—." The messenger's red face twitched and he choked as in terror.

"Altara!" The name reechoed weirdly from a dozen dry throats, and Nelson saw the skin suddenly pale and tighten over Hero John's face.

"What of the divine Altara, fool?" he thundered in a dreadful, shaken monotone. "Have those foul swine of Jarmuth dared—?"

"Forgive, oh Hero!" cried the groveling courier, his long red hair sweeping the marble floor. "The dog-sired Jereboam hath made proclamation in Jezreel that the Sacred Virgin is doomed to perish on the altar of Beelzebub, their demon god, in two days' time!"

"What?" The great marble-walled chamber was shaken by an unearthly outcry as horror and rage struggled for mastery in the circle of tense faces surrounding the momentarily forgotten aviators.

Bedlam broke loose, while Hero Giles sat as though stunned, staring on the shivering runner at his feet.

Nelson, very much on the alert, could see that the announcement of Altara's impending death had produced nothing short of a cataclysm in the plans of the council.

LIKE men paralyzed by electric shocks, the yellow bearded veterans and nobles sat stupefied, frozen in their last gesture. Then, in the midst of their silent despair, came the sound of a curious, high-pitched horn that had in its note something of the eery wail of a fire siren. The effect was magical, for the nobles sprang up, hands on sword hilts and eyes searching the corridor.

"The priests!" gasped a short, broad-shouldered noble at Altorius' left. "By Poseidon! 'Tis the fanfare of the Herakles himself."

Then indeed did the council glower, for, as Nelson soon learned, Herakles was the moving spirit and evil genius of that priestly party which had dared to imprison the Emperor.

Again the horn wailed its warning of the arch-priest's approach, whereat a stalwart hoplite in green painted armor clanked in, saluted stiffly and waited for Hero Giles' instructions.

"Bid the old man enter," directed the Prince at last. "Tell the graybeard he has naught to fear if he comes alone. Otherwise, bid him return to his kennel in the temples."

A moment after the hoplite had vanished, there appeared in the doorway a tall, emaciated old man on whose silvery head was set a curious golden mitre ending in the shape of a wondrously bejewelled trident. The curious Americans noted that the arch-priest's robes were as black as his evilly glittering eyes, and were embroidered with curious cabalistic symbols done in silver thread. In his withered hand Herakles carried a ceremonial trident—the mark of the Head Priest of Poseidon.

As though wary of advancing, the arch priest paused in the doorway, not three feet from where Nelson stood poised for action.

ALL at once the gaunt figure in black raised thin hands to the dome far overhead and cried in high-pitched prophetic tones:

"Woe to Atlans! When perishes Altara, virgin of Poseidon the God-head, then shall a darkness fall on Atlans! Her cities shall be cast down, there will be a weeping and wailing in the land, for Beelzebub and his followers shall prevail! Woe to Atlans and woe to ye all, blasphemous nobles!"

Gripped by a superstitious awe, the generals and nobles fell into an uneasy silence, fearfully lowering their eyes and then glancing askance at the plain khaki clad figures standing alert in their corner.

Nelson, defiantly meeting their eyes, beheld Hero Giles staring fixedly before him, his powerful shoulders bowed as though bearing an overwhelming burden.

Deeper grew the silence of disaster while the American furiously searched his mind for some means of thwarting the death in store for him and his companion. By chance, a word of Hero Giles recurred, the "pteranodons." What in the devil was a pteranodon? He turned sidewise to Alden who stood, hands in the pocket of his leather jacket, also thinking deeply.

"Dick," he whispered. "You studied paleontology at college. Do you remember what a pteranodon was?"

"A what?" The younger aviator seemed to make a definite effort to return to the present. "A pteranodon? I'm not sure, Vic, but I think it was a kind of flying reptile related to the pterodactyl group."

HE could go on no further, for Herakles, the arch-priest, raised his snowy head suddenly, his eyes blazing. "To save Atlans in her hour of trial, we demand that ye deliver to us the Wanderers. They shall die as an offering to Ares, God of War. Perchance he will preserve us." The arch-priest's deep-set and glittering eyes swept with venomous hatred the two calm-featured aviators, who looked very plain and unromantic in their flying jackets and khaki serge. "We, familiars of the Gods, herewith demand that the blasphemers perish on the War God's altar! Else shall ye all die unbeloved of the Gods!"

"And we do your bidding, will ye give us back His Splendor?" demanded Hero Giles.

"Nay—we priests do not bargain like hucksters."

Risking all, Nelson muttered a swift aside to Alden. "How big were those pteranodons?"

"Some species had a wing spread of twenty-five feet."

The muscular pilot's mouth closed into a firm, colorless line as he nodded and glanced at the vindictive old man who was by now white with fury.

Up sprang a good three-quarters of the nobles present and turned on the grim figure at the head of the board.

"Surrender the Wanderers!" they shouted. "We demand it!"

IN another instant the death sentence would have been forced on Hero Giles, but Victor Nelson leaped forward, pistol menacing the raging gray-bearded priest.

"Listen, all of you!" he shouted in deep tones that were strangely authoritative. "Beware, foolish Princes, how you threaten us. Great is our knowledge and power: you've seen that already. Even now, the other Wanderer and I can save or ruin Atlans, as we wish! Have ye forgotten the battle by Lake Copias?"

The Princes, furious at the American's defiance, half rose, hand on sword hilt, but sank back at a swift, menacing gesture from Nelson's pistol.

"What sayest thou, mad fellow?" screeched the arch-priest, his black eyes bright as knife points. "Save Atlans—?" Fierce questioning was in his sombre, sunken eyes.

"I said," repeated Nelson, "that, if we choose, we can yet save your Altara and the Emperor from death."

"Impossible! He is mad!" shouted Paul, the one-eyed Hero. "Not the Gods themselves could rescue Altara from the claws of the demon Beelzebub!" The nearest nobles flung themselves back in their chairs and snarled threats of all kinds as they gripped their sword hilts.

Sensing an inescapable climax, the khaki-clad American raised his pistol, covering Hero Paul, the speaker. "Silence!" he rasped. "You're a thick-headed idiot not to see the truth. Can this priest save Altara? No! You know damned well he can't! And yet you'd have us killed."

"Now, Herakles," he swung on the priest, "about this Altara matter—if you'll restore Altorius unharmed, guarantee our safety, and punish those liars who condemned us to death, the other Wanderer and I will undertake to not only prevent the sacrifice of Altara, but to bring the Princess back as well!"

TO all this Alden listened with increasing and indescribable dismay, his blue eyes round as marbles. "My God!" he whispered in an undertone. "What in the devil is Vic doing? *Undertake* is *right*, the crazy fool!"

"How will ye accomplish this mad boast?" demanded the arch-priest in deep suspicion. "Know ye that the Sacred Virgin lies captive in the dungeons of the great temple of Beelzebub? Know ye that this temple is in the center of Jezreel, capitol of Jarmuth?"

"I had some idea that was the case."

"Know ye," continued, the graybeard priest, "that Altara is ever guarded by two thousand picked priests and warriors? Know ye, moreover, that this vile sacrifice will be made but two days hence?"

The aviator's lean, dark head inclined with a serenity he far from felt.

At this point the scarred veteran officer who had spoken before broke in, his face menacing. "Believe not this liar, oh Hero Giles! He speaks with a tongue made bold by fear. He promises that which he cannot accomplish!"

Had Victor Nelson had time to reflect upon the weirdness of the plan he had evolved, he would probably have silently admitted that his grizzled accuser was more than a little justified, but as it was he smiled serenely.

From all sides rose a threatening shout. "Let the blasphemers be sacrificed. Ares will protect us!"

HIS yellow brows knit, Hero Giles wavered, but as he hesitated there ran through a great circular window a distant yet menacing shout. "Down with Altorius, the Unlucky! Down with the sons of Hudson! Give back to the ancient Gods their Sacred Virgin. Hail to Ares! Death to the Wanderers! Death! Death!"

Drowning out these ominous cries there came from below the window the brazen clang of trumpets and the clank of many armored men hurrying forward. Presently the mob's outcry grew fainter, but still the cries of "Death" could be heard.

It was a tense moment. Would Hero Giles remain friendly? With poignant anxiety, Nelson watched that dishevelled martial head sink forward in perplexity.

"Hero Giles," he warned, in a low voice. "You'd better trust us. You're risking nothing."

Slowly, the fierce blue eyes of the veteran rose, and, meeting the level gray ones of the aviator, lingered there as though asking a question. Suddenly reaching a determination, he rose to his feet and addressed the triumphantly grinning arch-priest, who tightly clutched his trident wand with thin, blue-veined fingers.

"Hearken, black crow of a priest, who has dared lay foul hands on His Splendor, the Emperor. This is my reply: show me how ye will rescue Altara; otherwise begone! My hand itches for the sword."

A DEEP silence fell while Herakles glowered helplessly, then shrewdly avoided the trap. "This is blasphemy!" he croaked and raised a quivering forefinger in solemn warning. "Woe to thee, Hero Giles. Woe to the people! Fear the wrath of the Gods!

"Jeer not, ye nobles!" Herakles stormed on. "Be not deceived by lies! I bid thee deliver these magicians to Ares, God of War!"

A nasty moment; Nelson's heart drummed as he gazed down at the row of uneasy, war-like faces, but Hero Giles proved the strength of his heritage. Back went his patrician head; he drew himself up to full height and stared coldly upon the black robed priest, who, nothing daunted, gave back look for look.

"Nay! We keep them: they will bear out their promise. I give ye good day, oh Holiness!"

Quivering with rage Herakles raised his withered hand in anathema. "Then perish, blind spawn of Hudson! Verily shall ye all die under the torture. Woe! Woe! Woe!"

Then, amid a strained silence, pregnant of distrust and disaster, the old man wheeled and stalked out.

As he watched the departure, color drained from the Atlantean prince's haggard features. "Ah," he observed bitterly, "ever have these black crows feasted on our land, and ever as birds of ill omen." He turned and, with a weary sigh, surveyed the group of loyal, but anxious souls. "I thank ye. Will ye still do my bidding and help to save our sovereign lord?"

Out flashed the swords of a dozen-odd nobles as they raised the hoarse, ringing cry of "Altorius! Altorius! Supreme!"

A LITTLE later Nelson, before a very mistrustful gathering composed of Hero Giles, Hero John and two or three other veterans, traced the barest outline of his plan.

"You understand? I'm to be taken to the border as a prisoner; then, in plain sight of the enemy lines, the guards must maltreat me and turn me loose."

The aviator searched one after another of the brutal, war-like faces, while Hero Giles translated for the benefit of two Atlantean generals who did not speak the royal language.

"Are you positive," Alden demanded of Hero John, "that this revolution in Atlans will die out if Altara is returned?"

"Yes! A thousand times yes!" The prince's fine eyes gleamed with savage enthusiasm. "With the Sacred Virgin restored to Atlans, new courage will come into the phalanxes! The priests will cease their outcries against them. Then, with the help of the blue maxima vapor, we will rend the dog-begotten followers of Jereboam limb from limb!"

"All right." Nelson's wiry khaki-clad body bent far over the table. "Remember, Hero Giles, that part of the fighting's up to you. When I'm gone, you'll do exactly what Alden tells you. Now, one thing more: what part of the border is still unquestionably loyal?"

Hero Giles frowned and shrugged his armor-clad shoulders a little helplessly beneath the splendid cloak of imperial green. "The gods alone know; but at the third division of this morning, Mayda and Thebes still vowed their loyalty. 'Tis there are quartered the phalanxes of the Imperial guards. They alone can I trust to the death."

"All right." Bending over a huge parchment map of the valley, Nelson nodded, and his keen black eyes became very serious. "I want you to concentrate every man you can muster in each of those cities. Meanwhile tell the populace..." He drew a deep breath. "...that Altara will certainly be returned to them."

"Art thou sure?" broke in the scarred veteran in the dented breast plate; then, his brow dark with doubt, he engaged Hero Giles and the rest in a heated, low-voiced colloquy.

ALDEN stepped near, an anxious frown on his unshaven features. "Think this idea of yours is sure-fire?"

"No," Nelson's lean head shook. "I'm far from sure. It's a wild gamble at best, but we can't be any worse off than we are now. If the priests win out, we're sunk and no mistake about it; but there's a fighting chance my idea could be brought off."

"Now look here," objected the younger pilot tensely. "What's this rot about your going into Jarmuth alone? How d'you know they won't skin you alive once you're over the border?"

"I don't," admitted his friend, shrugging slightly. "But I don't see there's anything but to take the risk. If I don't go over there, sure as shooting we're going to feed some damn unpleasant kind of beast here in Atlans.

"Another thing," Nelson said, turning to the Hero who, surrounded by the others, was bent in deep consultation over a map. "How am I to know Altara if I see her? Is there a statue, a painting or something—?"

The Hero's aquiline features lit in a slow smile. "Nay, we have better than that. Come, thou shalt see the Sacred Virgin as she now is."

The members of the conference followed Hero Giles down a short corridor, through a couple of doors and into a chamber where a huge disc of crystal stood on edge fixed upon an axis above a bewildering array of wires, pipes and gauges.

HERO John, who seemed familiar with the mechanism, turned a lever, whereupon the disc commenced to spin like a pie plate on a dance floor. Faster and faster it spun, silently gathering speed each second while a low humming sound filled the chamber. Gradually the outline of the whirling disk commenced to brighten, tinting the scar-seamed, craggy features of the Atlantean generals and picking glorious, glowing lights from the jewels on Hero Giles' wonderfully engraved breastplate.

"Ah." Hero John turned a small dial. "The crystal warms. Look, oh Wanderers!"

Nelson rubbed his eyes incredulously, for in the heart of the shimmering circle had materialized the outline of a room with walls of yellow marble.

"Well, I'm damned!" gasped Alden. "See how it flickers!"

As the revolving disc of crystal gained top speed, the flickering subsided and a picture, clearer than most photographs, could be seen in the center. A wondrously slender, yellow-haired young girl clad in Grecian robes of pale blue sat in deep despond upon a plain wooden couch, with a black haired servant kneeling before her, apparently lacing sandals on her tiny, pink-hued feet.

"Bring closer the face," snapped Hero Giles gruffly.

Gradually the focus changed, like the close-up of a movie camera, until in the center of the madly whirling disc could be seen in minute detail and living color the face of an indescribably lovely girl.

"Whew," muttered Nelson, staring in silent amazement. "No wonder they want her back! She makes Ziegfeld's little girls look like Armenian refugees." He cast a sidewise glance, but Alden had apparently not heard him; the younger American stood gazing with rapturous joy at the girl.

"Aye! Aye!" The two veteran generals uttered stifled groans and one of them drew a hand across his eyes. "Poseidon save her! Aye! Preserve the fair Altara."

"Wouldst thou not doubly save her, now?" demanded Hero John in a low voice that bespoke his anguish. He seemed suddenly older than the grim, helmeted veterans to either side.

"You bet! I guess a man sees a face like that only once is a lifetime. And now," Nelson continued with an effort to return to the practical, "there's no time to be lost—so I'd just like to take a look at those pteranodons of yours."

A FEW minutes later, the two aviators found themselves nearing a lofty structure which adjoined the imperial palace. It was constructed along the lines of an immense aviary. Between beautiful, glistening Ionic columns of white marble, gleamed bronze bars, set at regular intervals to prevent the escape of the most appalling creatures which could ever have skimmed the air.

"What in the devil is your idea?" demanded Alden, taken aback. "God, look at the loathsome brutes!"

Some of these huge, flying reptiles were hopping awkwardly over the ground picking at bones and refuse littering the floor with long pelican-like bills, which were, however, very much thicker than those of pelicans, and set with sharp teeth at least six inches long.

"Not very pretty are they? Kind of look like huge bats," commented Nelson thoughtfully. "Wonder if they could be handled?"

"Yes, their wings are a bit on the leathery side. Look at 'em up yonder." Alden pointed to the roof of that immense aviary where, hanging head downwards like gigantic bats, must have been hundreds upon hundreds of the pteranodons. One of them, whistling oddly, fluttered up to the bars, affording the Wanderers an excellent view of a loathsome head, the back of which ended in a curious sort of horn, that, projecting backwards, jutted far above its rear. Fierce, vermillion eyes with green irises glared at the Americans through the bars, and great wings of greasy-looking leather fanned a disgusting stench from the interior of the aviary.

"SWEET little things," was Alden's comment. "Good heavens! Try to imagine having one of those great things swooping down on you. Hey, Alden, look at that big devil over there! He must have a wing spread of thirty feet. Big as a Moth plane, isn't he?"

For answer the pteranodon clattered its vast beak savagely. One of the generals stooped and, catching up a huge slab of meat from a basket nearby, hurled it through the bars into the gaping jaws.

"What would ye with these creature?" demanded Hero Giles with undisguised curiosity.

"You'd be surprised." Nelson was not deliberately rude, but his mind was wrapped up in the daring project he had evolved. "I want a couple of the biggest of these caught and set aside in a courtyard where there will be no one looking on. If your people can train and handle podokos and allosauri—I guess a couple of Yanks ought to be able to manage these flying nightmares. So don't you worry about us."

Hero Giles uttered grim, significant laugh. "Thou hadst best manage them. I note yonder pteranodon is in need of nourishment."

CHAPTER TEN

WITH sharp anxiety, Victor Nelson kept watching the towers of Jezreel rise ever clearer above the great, warm plain of Jarmuth, but, for all that, he noted how distinctly Jezreel differed from Heliopolis. The Jarmuthian capital was predominantly amber-yellow instead of white in color; its towers were flat-topped, angular, hideous structures that compared not at all favorably with the graceful Grecian architecture of Atlantean public buildings.

The populace, he decided, as he strode along in the midst of half a dozen silent guards, were as harsh and graceless as their architecture. Whereas the Atlanteans had been white skinned and uniformly red haired—save for those of Hudsonian blood—the inhabitants of Jarmuth almost without exception were black haired and had dark, olive-hued skins.

"They're the lost tribes of Israel, all right," Nelson decided after a brief sojourn in that savage land lying beyond Apidanus—the great boiling river, whose bubbling and scalding currents had for centuries served as a natural boundary between the two realms. But now the Jarmuthian armies had crossed it and were steadily pushing back the demoralized and despairing Atlanteans with savage energy that heaped the dead in hillocks.

"Their armor," mused the ragged, barefoot prisoner, studying his silent guards, "looks a lot like a Roman legionnaire's, but that six pointed star on their helmets is pure Semitic. Yes, this sure is an Asiatic outfit."

His eyes wandered from one fierce, big-nosed infantryman to another and noted the splendid physical structure of the majority. Evidently hardier, much less refined and luxury-loving than the Atlanteans, these swart warriors disdained robes and other garments. Save for helmet, armor and brief black kilts, they were quite naked. Like the Atlantean hoplites the infantrymen carried spears, steam retortii and quantities of grenades.

The country side through which the prisoner passed had a holiday air, for garlands of flowers hung in every doorway, and naked, pot-bellied children squatted by the roadside, industriously weaving crowns and streamers of gay blossoms.

"Look, Atlantean dog!" commanded the black-bearded leader of the escort. "Let thine infidel eyes gaze upon the mightiest city of the world. Seest thou yonder Ziggurat which o'er towers all others?"

Nelson raised eyes red-rimmed from sleeplessness and deep anxiety—for the crafty Jarmuthians had proved unexpectedly unwilling to credit him as the Atlantean outcast and would-be renegade he had pretended to be.

"Yes," he said in reply to the English-speaking *jehar's*—captain's—question. "What's it for?"

"'Tis the temple of the almighty Beelzebub, Steam God of Jarmuth. Without his hot breath no wheel would turn, our armies would be powerless and this land would perish under the ice of the outer world." The dark eyed officer's eye fell speculatively upon his bound and dust-covered prisoner. "Perchance, dog of a spy, thou wilt die during to-day's fourth division* together with Altara, pale daughter of the feeble, false god Poseidon."

THIS afternoon?

Nelson could not realize that the time had flown so quickly. Four short hours separated him from the crisis of his life. A thousand doubts assailed him. What if Alden or Hero Giles failed in their share of the great scheme for rescue? Narrowly, the aviator's eye searched the great, rich plain, then swept the amber-hued sky where, far above the plain, Jilboa, the nearest flame sun, beat off the Arctic chill and darkness.

The great, black-bearded jehar eased the straps from which was suspended the brass coil of his retortii. "Aye," he chuckled, his thick lips parted in a crafty smile. "Ere long will the fair flesh of Altara grace the ceremonial board of His Exaltation, the King, and his priests and princes."

Nelson gasped in horror. The divinely beautiful Altara—butchered for meat like a calf? Grotesque! Ghastly! "What! You eat your prisoners?" He felt sick, nauseated.

For answer, the swart Jarmuthian raised an enormous hand and dealt the captive American a stinging cuff which made his teeth rattle.

"Peace!" he snarled. "Else I slit thy spying throat ere we pass yonder walls."

---

*The Atlantean day was divided into six divisions of four hours each; due to the flame suns there was no sunrise or sunset.

Fingering a short blue-black beard that was frizzed into tight curls in the Assyrian manner, the jehar lengthened his stride as the little detachment clanked into the shadow of a great wall surrounding Jezreel, and through a huge gate guarded by two hideous, jackal-headed effigies.

Hurrying into the city were throngs of eager men, women and children, interspersed with muscular, black bearded soldiers who cast threatening, baleful eyes on the pale-skinned prisoner.

AT first the great metropolis of Jezreel seemed boundless, for everywhere arose tall, massive monuments of yellow marble whose facades were engraved with Sanskrit characters, thus bearing out Nelson's surmise that this was indeed a race of Semitic origin.

Here and there hurried grey-bearded, vulture-eyed priests oddly garbed in corrupt Occhive and Tyrian regalia. Nelson found it odd to see the Tablet of the Laws, which Jarmuth so openly ignored, swaying on their yellow robed breasts; and none cried out more menacingly nor more loudly against the limping, wan-faced captive, than these same ecclesiastics, who must have long since forgotten all worship of Jehovah in the foul service of a bestial golden effigy.

A stone sailed through the air, narrowly missing the American; then another, which struck his shoulder.

"God, what a rough looking crowd," thought Nelson, as the guards, cursing, held back the screaming mob. "At this rate I won't live to even reach the temple!"

Every second his life stood in great danger. Unkempt, sloe-eyed women hurled themselves, shrieking with fury, against the armored chests of the guards, who were hard pressed to beat them off with their spear hafts.

Nelson's one small ray of comfort in this evil hour was the fact that his .45 pistol remained untouched in a food wallet. At the border the jehar had cast one contemptuous glance at the weapon, but, no doubt deeming it some strange culinary tool, he had made no effort to remove it.

It was a continual struggle for the guards to win their way up a long flight of stairs, for ever the great stream of humanity grew denser and more menacing.

NELSON felt a violent sense of revolt grip his being. "I must win free," he thought. "If I fail, Alden dies, and—and—" For the first time he realised how much he wanted to actually see Altara. Like a clear cameo, an image of her had remained fresh in his memory. Except for her Grecian garments she might have been a lovely, carefree English or American girl.

"And these decadent swine would sacrifice her!" The thought was sickening. Yet how could he prevent the pitiful tragedy?

Fortunately, a detachment of troops—tall, sinewy fellows with conical helmets, crested with six-pointed stars—reenforced the guards just as clawing hands began to snatch and tug at the prisoner's ragged Atlantean chiton of blue cotton.

Almost before he realized it, Nelson was dragged inside a great gloomy building and into a circular chamber where four eagle-featured elders sat in council beneath the six-pointed star of Sem. On approaching, the jehar in command sank on one knee and in humble salute raised both hands to the tribunal.

"A tough looking desk sergeant they've got," muttered the prisoner to himself as his eye met the chilling regard of a lean, yellow-faced priest. "Wonder what I'm booked for?" Idiotically, he recalled being summoned before a traffic court, years back. "Guess I don't get off with vagrancy; it'll probably be everything from speeding to mayhem, with maybe arson and well-poisoning thrown in."

The deliberations of this ominous court proved to be appallingly short. The dour-faced elders merely put their heads together, muttered a few sentences, then straightened up almost immediately. The chief priest—he with the yellow face—thrust out his fist and made the immemorial signal of death by jerking his thumb at the black marble floor.

BEFORE the outraged and astounded aviator could utter a word of protest, powerful guards seized and hauled him off down a dark, narrow passageway in which the fetid prison smell was very strong. Too wise to struggle against overwhelming odds, yet appalled at the thought of his impending doom, Nelson was dragged into a room where four or five furtive, enslaved Atlanteans, made dumb by the removal of their tongues, were engaged in a curious occupation.

On a bare stone bench, five other Atlantean captives were sitting in miserable silence. They made a grotesque array, for their heads were crowned with gay yellow and blue flowers, and the upper half of their perfectly formed bodies gleamed with an application of a sweet-smelling oil. About their wrists and waists were twined fragrant garlands of yellow roses which hid the leather straps confining their hands.

Struggling, Nelson was forced on to the bench, whereupon slaves, skipping to avoid the lash of a scarred, olive-hued slave driver, hurried to wash the newly arrived prisoner's limbs, face and hands. A weary-looking old slave with sunken, rheumy eyes listlessly pulled the blue chiton from Nelson's broad shoulders, and would have removed the food pouch had not the prisoner winked vigorously. The ministering slave glanced swiftly sidewise and, discovering the slave driver's attention directed to another corner, pulled the upper folds of the chiton over the food pouch and its precious contents, then set a crown of yellow roses more or less askew on the American's head. For all the peril of the situation Nelson could not suppress a fleeting smile as the phrase, "For I'm to be Queen of the May, Mother," leaped nonsensically into his brain.

"YES, I guess they are getting us all dolled up for a sacrifice of some kind." Nelson's heart began to pound at the thought. Then he fought for self control. It must be a hideously realistic nightmare! He, Victor Nelson, American citizen, a quiet birdman, member of the Caterpillar Club and ex-flight commander of the A. E. F. was about to be offered as a sacrifice to some hideous, pagan god? Nonsense! He'd wake up in a minute and hear the drone of a ship on the line.

He blinked, staring fixedly at a single ray of light that came streaming in through a small, barred window, then glanced sidewise at his fellow victims, who with Spartan indifference sat waiting for the end of all things. It was no dream!

From the tiny window came the shrill discordant braying of many trumpets, and a roar like that of a football crowd arose surprisingly near. In response, the slave driver lashed the gaudily bedecked sacrificial victims to their feet with vicious cuts of his pliant whip, and herded them like a drove of calves down a very long passage, lit at intervals by those strange column lamps of incandescent gas. In their red glare the doomed six seemed as though already bathed in blood.

"Must be some crowd of people outside," muttered Nelson as a great gale of sound deafened him. Yonder the amber glare of the flame suns glimmered, and now it was his turn to step into the open!

ON a sort of spiral roadway he paused, breathless, awed, bewildered, for there, eddying restlessly about the bases of towers and other huge structures, was a great sea of up-turned faces. To his surprise he found the passage he had followed opened perhaps halfway up what must be the great Ziggurat of Beelzebub. He judged the tower's height must be immense, for already the crowd was a good hundred feet below.

*"Zarotoa! Zarotoa! ù Wlanka!"**

Nelson shivered. How terrible was the wild, bloodthirsty clamor of that massive throng, when they

---

*Death to the victims!

beheld the six flower-decked prisoners appear upon the circular winding road which led to the lofty and wind-swept summit of the great conical pyramid of the people of Jezreel.

And behind the victims marched eighteen or twenty spearmen gorgeously uniformed in yellow and black painted armor. Their retortii were plated with gold, and in the center of a star forming the crest of each helmet was set a diamond large as a hickory nut.

Preceding the despairing prisoners marched a squad of tall, clean-shaven priests with great gold hoops in their ears. They blew mightily upon long, curved horns, and were followed by perhaps a dozen lithe, posturing girls, half clothed in diaphanous yellow robes. These priestesses swung golden censers which flung bluish clouds of aromatic smoke high into the humid air above.

UP and up, around and around the great tower temple, Nelson was dragged, while the vast city of Jezreel, palaces, towers, courts, dwellings and all, lay like a great panorama below. Up and up, and the wind grew stronger while Nelson marvelled at the great height of the structure he was mounting. Immediately in front of him swayed the naked shoulders of the three captive Atlanteans; he could see rose petals from their crowns fluttering in the strong warm breeze sweeping that man-made pinnacle for the worship of a heathen god.

Despairingly, the American's eyes searched the horizon, to discover nothing but a few great birds wheeling lazily in the bronze-hued sky. Very clearly he could discern three of the flame suns, casting flame high from their peaks.

"Alden!" he groaned. "Oh God, Alden, don't fail me!"

Chilled by the fate in store, he scanned the dark and hostile faces below, but found no friendly visage.

Up and up. The procession was now nearing the summit.

There were hosts of poignant problems before him, each vital if Altara and the Empire of Atlans were to be saved; but one primary question immediately confronted him. How could he get his hands free? He ventured a few words in English to the stolid Atlantean at his side, whereat the fellow only stared dully and shook his red, flower-crowned head.

He next tried to cautiously work loose his hands, but to no avail. The rope of plaited skin binding his aching wrists together was tough as any rawhide. Cursing, he abandoned the effort, and, as his eyes once more swept the great bloodthirsty throng below, he felt himself doomed indeed.

CHAPTER ELEVEN

STANDING at last on the summit of the great Ziggurat, Nelson found himself staring up at the fearsome golden image of the dread demon Beelzebub. The god stood some twelve feet in height and had a hideous human face, but, in place of hair and beard, countless golden tubes writhed in all directions. From the end of one, the puzzled prisoner beheld several tiny feathers of steam creeping forth, indicating that these hairs were a species of steam vent.

When, with the other captives, he was commanded to halt near its base, he further discovered that the idol sat upon an incredible throne of yellow marble, the sides of which were carved with a myriad of Sanskrit characters, necessarily quite meaningless to the seemingly doomed aviator.

In a grim and silent rank before Beelzebub's feet, stood some six or eight priest-executioners bending their black-robed bodies against the strong wind which swept that ghastly pinnacle.

Just below the base of the image, Nelson noted several great, copper coils. These coils were no doubt conducting steam from the interior of the Ziggurat. Between the knees of Beelzebub rested a huge, shallow bowl, the use of which puzzled the American not a little, for he saw that the base of this ornate receptacle was also wrapped with a number of steam coils. Two great hands, ending in cruel-looking claws, were stretched horizontally above the demon's knees, seeming to plead for victims.

SUDDENLY a deep toned brazen gong sounded somewhere below; the trumpeters blew an ear-piercing note; and, at a gesture from the high priest, four of the brawny executioner-priests leaped forward, seized one of the Atlantean victims, hurled him to the stone platform and, in an unbelievably short interval, strapped the shrieking wretch by wrists, elbows, knees and ankles to a long, brass rod. Slung like a dead deer from a rail, they lifted the helpless Atlantean, and, while five hundred thousand voices roared in acclaim the priests fitted the pole ends into notches above the hands of the idol with the effect that the idol actually seemed to be clutching its victim.

Then, from all the pipes composing the hair and beard of Beelzebub, sprang forth hissing spouts of snowy steam which, whipped by the rising wind, went whirling madly down the lee of the Ziggurat. At the same time, from the half open mouth of the demon issued a fearful, screaming howl, a thousand times louder than the whistle of a speeding locomotive. Deafening and barbaric, it was reechoed from a hundred towers and battlements.

A dreadful, exultant well burst from the multitude below as the red-robed priest drew from beneath his garments a sickle-shaped knife that glittered evilly in the light of the flaming suns. Still chanting, he stooped and quickly made a deep incision over the heart of the victim. While a piercing, agonized shriek burst from the ashen lips of the doomed Atlantean, his bright life-blood began to splash into the golden bowl below where, due to the presence of the steam coils, it swiftly commenced to hiss and bubble. Very quickly the last scarlet drops had fallen.

Then while Nelson, sick and horrified, stood watching, the dead body on its pole was taken down, unstrapped, and hurled, limp and red-spattered, to the next lower platform where other priests waited to dismember it for the ceremonial cannibalism soon to follow.

IN rapid succession two more victims were slaughtered amid the blood-hungry cheers of the Jarmuthian populace. Now the great bowl hissed and bubbled with a generous supply of the dark red fluid, from which rose clouds of evil-smelling steam that fanned the hideous features above.

Suddenly from below there arose an excited shout far mightier and louder than any that had preceded it, when the executioners, sweating profusely from their vile exertions, now turned and, spying Nelson, hurried forward. Coincidently, the American's tightly bound hands disappeared beneath the chiton. Squaring his shoulders, he gripped the pistol, prepared to make a good end.

"They'll get me, but before I die I'll send at least two or three of these devils to hell," he thought. "Come on—"

However, for some bit of inexplicable reasoning, the arch-priest beckoned back his satellites, while roar upon roar of terrific excitement swelled from the swarming mob below, and a shout which at last became distinguishable bid fair to split the heavens. "Altara! Altara! Altara!"

Slowly, the temporarily reprieved victim's muscles stiffened. He understood. The next victim was to be the fair Altara, sister of Altorius and Sacred Virgin of Atlans.

"Altara! Altara!" A rising hurricane of impassioned human voices thundered the name.

Suddenly, the desire to live burned doubly strong in the American's breast. He must somehow prevent this inhuman catastrophe. But how? How?

Stealing a quick glance over his shoulder, Nelson stifled a groan. The southern horizon remained clear, and put an end to hope. No help! He must fight it out to the end alone.

A RANK of exultant, black-bearded priests now appeared at the head of the stairway, then a quartet of olive skinned, semi-naked priestesses joyfully clashing brass cymbals.

There came an interval—and Nelson's heart stood still as there appeared the lovely head and shoulders of her whom he had first seen in the heart of the revolving crystal. Even more fiercely, mad revolt at fate gripped him.

Through hot, strained eyes the American saw that the stately Altara was beautiful beyond all possible comparison, and that she seemed utterly unafraid in the hour of her dreadful death. The Atlantean maiden's large, clear blue eyes were fixed with calm resignation on the distant flame sun of Jilboa. On her curling golden hair had been set a circlet of ceremonial yellow roses, while her white, slender body was thinly covered with a scanty robe of yellow silk.

Slowly, and moving her small bare feet in a regal stride, Altara climbed the last few steps and stood straight and unafraid before the hideous demon god of Jarmuth.

Thousands of frantic inner voices assailed the aviator's consciousness. "Save her! You must save her! She's too young, too beautiful to die!"

Like a vast maelstrom of sound, so swelled the lustful cry of the dark multitude at the base of the Ziggurat, while the arch-priest chanted his litany in a sort of triumphant exultation. Then, all at once, one of the executioners roughly tripped the golden haired girl, sprawling her helpless on the bloody stones; and, before Nelson could quite realize it, the slender, silver hued form lay limp and helpless between Beelzebub's bloody claws.

LIKE a dynamo furiously gathering speed, so buzzed Nelson's brain. He was going to save her—if only for a brief interval! One man against a nation. Through a raging mist of fury he saw the red-robed priest raise his lean arms; then the American's bound hands darted beneath the blue chiton to reappear immediately. No one saw the pistol, for every eye was rivetted upon the gleaming, sickle-knife of the red priest. Like a voice from hell, that eery scream burst again from Beelzebub's throat as his priest stepped near, the knife raised.

Amid a deafening roar the sickle-knife flashed higher; but it never fell, for the red priest suddenly reeled, clutched his chest and, staring wildly, staggered sidewise, while the assembled priests stared thunderstruck. The deafening roar of Beelzebub, the clamor of horns and cymbals had drowned out the report. In superstitious awe the Jarmuthians leaped back, panic-stricken, from the convulsively writhing body of the red priest, which rolled crazily down the steps before the idol; but a high shout of terror rang out as he toppled off the summit and, like a discarded puppet, plunged down the precipitous side of the cone-like tower.

Again Nelson's pistol spat, and two of the executioners collapsed in kicking agony. Like an avenging fury, the American raged about the summit, the pistol in his bound bands dealing death right and left until panic seized the remaining priests, who, with one accord, abandoned their weapons to rush headlong down the dizzy, winding roadway. In a trice, none but Altara, Nelson, the two Atlanteans and the fallen priests remained on the summit.

IT was the work of a moment for the Atlanteans to cast loose Nelson's bound wrists, and he theirs; time was precious, for, from below, a furious cohort of spearmen were charging up the stairs, their dark features terrible in their wrath.

"Only four more shots!" The sickening realization dashed into Nelson's brain. "That'll never stop them." Then in the midst of his despair he saw an answer. Stepping back he fired twice full into the great steam coil circling the base of the idol.

Spang! Spang! His bullets smacked through the copper coil to puncture neat, round holes. As he fervently hoped, jets of live steam rushed through these vents with terrible force and bathed the head of the stairs with a scalding, blinding vapor. Howling like mad beasts, the agonized Jarmuthian hoplites fell back, while overhead Beelzebub bellowed incessantly, shaking the sky with his hideous voice.

"That's better." But Nelson knew his triumph to be brief. *"Where in hell is Alden?"* he raged as with shaking hands he released the bewildered girl from the death bar after the two Atlanteans had lifted it and its fair burden from the claws of Beelzebub.

Picking up the swords and other weapons of the fallen priests the two Atlanteans uttered their deep-toned war cry of *Halor vàn!* and joyously prepared to die fighting, as furious roar on roar of wrath arose from the populace, infuriated at being cheated of their prey. But the black-armored temple guards dared not charge those twin steam jets barring their approach. Accordingly they tried other means.

NELSON'S heart nearly stopped as a small, ominous object sailed up quickly from below and clattered on the platform. It was a grenade. With the lightning speed of thought, the American kicked it to the landing below, where it detonated, the explosion annihilating a detachment of Jarmuthians by drenching them with the terrible fungus gas. His heart bounding with savage joy, Nelson watched the deadly green fog leap from the broken grenade and of its own accord settle on the nearest soldiers. With the usual astonishing speed there formed upon the stricken soldiers below that poisonous yellow mould, whose fungus-like shoots sprouted through nostrils and mouths. On the dense crowd below the bomb's effect was appalling, and no more grenades were hurled...

During the respite Nelson's anguished eyes once more swept the skies. He started. Was it true or was it a mirage? Far to the southward a small, black speck materialized in the orange-hued heavens. Good old Alden! Hope wavered in the American's breast. Could he and his two fellows beat off the infuriated Jarmuthians long enough? He doubted it.

A shower of spears sailed up, but because of the angle, their trajectory was too great, and like rays of death the lances flashed harmlessly overhead to plunge over the summit and wreak death among those on the other side.

Nearer and nearer came the black speck while from the populace a low shout of amazement arose. Coincidently Nelson's heart stopped; aghast, he saw that the steam was no longer hissing from the holes at the idol's feet! Evidently, the steam current had been shut off from below to allow the raging priests to lead their followers in a desperate charge up the stairs.

Marshalling an Atlantean to either side, Nelson sprang to the head of the stair and fired full in the face of gorgeously robed priests who staggered back screaming. But the others wavered only an instant.

"*Halor vàn!*" Both Atlanteans hurled spears retrieved from the abandoned weapons—and each struck down his man.

THE American's eye flickered up. Yes, there came a strange, but welcome sight: a great creature with enormous, leathery pinions was circling down towards the tower top! A clashing of weapons brought Nelson's eyes earthwards. He joined in a furious melée at the stair top, like the Atlanteans, using a captured bronze sword. There came a deep groan as the right-hand Atlantean collapsed with a bloodied bronze spear point standing far out from between his naked shoulder blades.

A swooping shadow fell across the slowly advancing attackers. Beholding that awesome creature the Jarmuthians cowered, hesitated; then in headlong panic they darted below, uttering howls of fear and pursued by the surviving Atlantean, who, gone berserk, must have shortly paid for his folly.

The pteranodon was now quite recognizable, and seated on a double saddle was Alden, skillfully guiding the ungainly monster by means of a curious bridle, by shifting his weight and by pressing certain nerve centers between the great reptile's leathery shoulders.

Down, down circled Alden until the great wings skimmed just above Beelzebub's ugly golden head.

Her courage strained beyond endurance, Altara screamed shrilly in fear as Alden guided the huge reptile to the summit and forced it to light.

"Quick!" shouted Alden. "They're coming back up!"

"All right!" Catching up the fainting girl, Nelson hurdled two or three fallen bodies, and, while Alden showered fungus bombs upon the returning Jarmuthians, he laid his precious burden across the saddle and secured her with straps specially designed for the purpose.

"All right, Dick," he snapped. "Get going!"

"But you?" Alden's brown face was terribly intent.

"I'm not going! This creature could never carry the three of us. It can't, I tell you! Hurry, those devils are coming!"

Alden folded his arms. "If you don't go, I don't."

"All right then," snarled Nelson, vaulting into the saddle after casting loose the inert, yellow-robed girl. "Be a damned fool! We'll all die now."

IT was a near thing, for the pteranodon, scenting the fresh blood, was very loath to obey its master, and scuffed awkwardly around the tower top two or three times, while Nelson, clutching Altara to him, expended his last shot in driving back the enemy.

At last, the pteranodon spread its huge brown pinions and took off. Then Nelson gasped in alarm, for, unaccustomed to the heavy weight it now bore, the pteranodon scaled earthwards with the speed of a meteor, wildly flapping its bat-like-wings. Down! Down! Nelson had an impression of people scattering like frightened ants.

Alden cursed, tugged furiously on the bridle, and set his weight back in the saddle, but to no avail. Down! Ever down! The pteranodon now struggled among the tall buildings.

A sickening sense of defeat gripped Nelson as a long jet of steam shot out from a huge brass retortii mounted on the roof of an arsenal. The scalding fingers of steam just missed its target, but fortunately served to sting the descending pteranodon. With a convulsive shudder and a whistling scream, the hideous reptile commenced to flap its gigantic wings faster, and, slowly but surely, began to rise over the yellow temples and towers of the barbarous city of Jezreel.

WHAT followed is now a matter of Atlantean history. On its pages is set forth in full detail how the giant pteranodon barely crossed the boiling river to sink exhausted in the outskirts of Tricca.

There, also, is described the series of tremendous battles in which the Atlanteans, led by Altorius and inspired by the return of their Sacred Virgin, employed the terrible fungus gas to overwhelm the Jarmuthian invaders, driving them back with great slaughter to the steaming plains of their own land.

At even greater length is described the great triumph Altorius accorded the victorious aviators on the occasion of Victor Nelson's marriage to Altara.

"Doth it not seem strange," she whispered as they stood looking out over the great, sleeping city of Heliopolis, "that thou of the New World and I of the Lost World, should stand man and wife?"

The American's tanned face softened. "My darling," he whispered, "there are lots of strange things in the new Atlantis—but this isn't one of them."

THE END

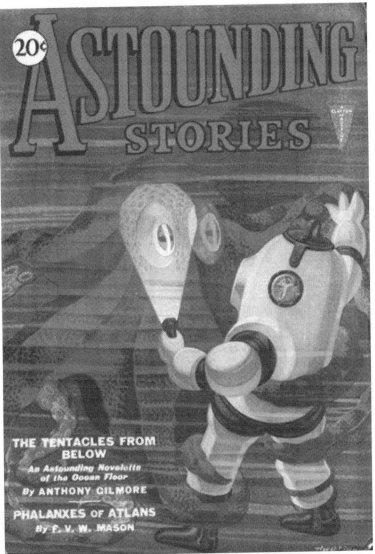

F. Van Wyck Mason's "Phalanxes of Atlans" was serialized in two issues of *Astounding Stories* in 1931. Part one appeared in the February issue.

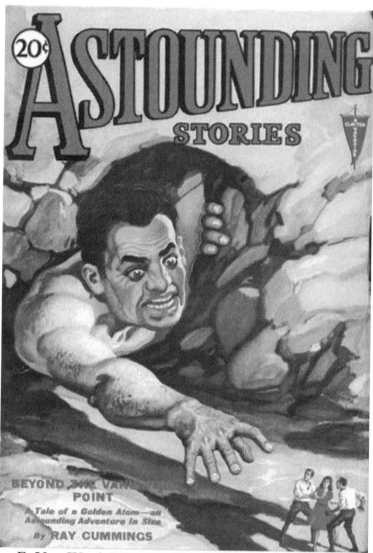

F. Van Wyck Mason's "Phalanxes of Atlans" was
serialized in two issues of *Astounding Stories* in 1931.
Part two appeared in the March issue.

Bonus Lost Race Story:
The People of the Pyramids

By
William P. McGivern

"COME, come," the fat, brown-skinned proprietor of the gaudy little shop in Cairo cried with more enthusiasm than coherence. "Lukka, lukka," he said proudly, waving a fat arm at the piles of merchandise stacked in the interior of his shop.

Neal Kirby grinned good-naturedly and allowed himself to be half-dragged, half-led into the establishment. He knew he was perfectly secure against the wiles of the fat shopkeeper for he only had one American dollar in his pocket. And his appetite had already staked a claim on that dollar for dinner.

With the proprietor pattering hopefully at his heels he browsed up and down the narrow aisles examining the ropes of cheap beads, the gayly colorful silks and satins and the thousand-and-one sleepy-looking Buddhas, of all sizes and shapes, that stared at him from the shelves.

He was turning to leave when a steely glitter in a corner caught his eye. Looking closely he saw that it was a narrow silver casket with a glass top that had caught the light. Through the glass top he could see a slim stiletto-like knife resting on a pad of red silk. Strangely, it excited his curiosity. He wondered vaguely

People of the PYRAMIDS

BY WILLIAM P. McGIVERN

A ball of flame lashed out at him from the pyramid's entrance

7here was no hidden city here, Neal Kirby knew. It must be a mirage. But men aren't murdered because of a vision!

why a piece of merchandise of such obvious value should be tucked away in the darkest corner of the shop.

"How much?" he asked, pointing to the casket. The proprietor shook his head until his fat jowls quivered like cups of jelly.

"No sale, no sale," he said breathlessly. He grabbed Neal by the arm. "Come, come," he waved to the displays on the opposite side of the shop. "Lukka, lukka."

Neal shook his head. Stubbornness had been added to his curiosity now. Disregarding the angry squeals of the fat shopkeeper, he bent and picked up the casket. Opening the casket, he almost gasped at the incredible beauty of the knife.

The blade, about eight inches long, gleamed as if it had been delicately forged from pure silver and the handle was formed in the shape of a man's torso, from some strange red metal that glowed with a fiery luminescence. A small, cunningly chiseled head topped the handle of the knife, and at the neckline where it joined the torso, it was circled by a cluster of small, but perfect diamonds.

Neal whistled in admiration. He was no judge of precious stones and metals but anyone could see that the knife would be worth a Rajah's ransom. So absorbed was he in the contemplation of the fabulously beautiful knife that he did not hear the sudden sharp exclamation that sounded from the wheezing proprietor. He didn't hear the footsteps behind him, but he did hear the quiet, sibilant voice that cut through the silence.

"Give me that knife!"

NEAL turned in surprise. Two people stood behind him. One was a man of medium height with a thin, arrogant face and sandy hair but Neal did not take time to notice anything else about him, for he was too busy staring in admiration at the girl who was with him.

She was tall, with hauntingly blue eyes, and fine blonde hair that cascaded in graceful waves almost to her shoulders. Her slender, charmingly feminine figure was accentuated by the smartly tailored white gabardine suit she wore. She looked cool and fresh and American.

Neal smiled suddenly. Just seeing a girl like this made him feel certain that Cairo was a fine place after all.

"It's a small world, isn't it?" he said to her.

She looked anxiously at the man she was with and murmured something under her breath that he didn't hear. Neal's smile faded as he looked closely at the girl. There was a hidden fear lurking in the depths of her eyes and he saw that the small handkerchief in her hands had been twisted into a small, crushed ball.

Her companion held out his hand imperiously.

"Will you give me the knife?" he snapped. "Or must I summon the police?"

Neal stiffened at the man's tone. There was something so definitely insulting in it that he felt a hot flush of anger staining his face. His big hands closed spasmodically over the knife in his hands.

"You might get better results," he suggested as coolly as he could, "if you'd stop snarling at people and improve your manners. The word 'please' can work wonders in a lot of cases. You might look it up some time."

The man swallowed a reply and his jaw clamped shut. His face had drained white and his small, steel blue eyes hardened into pinpoints of angry light.

"Will you give me that knife?" he almost whispered. His hand slipped slowly into the outside pocket of his coat, where a suspicious bulge showed.

Neal straightened slowly, his eyes narrowing to mere slits. He had not missed the gesture or its significance. In spite of the tenseness of the situation he was able to realize that the incident was strange in every respect. The man's rage and impatience were wholly unreasonable, completely out of proportion to the trifling affair. The girl was looking imploringly at her companion and her hands were clasped tensely together as if in silent supplication.

THE fat, waddling shopkeeper shoved himself between them at that instant, stammering breathless apologies. And as suddenly and abruptly as that the incident was over. The thin man with the arrogant face withdrew his hand from his pocket and went about the business of lighting a cigarette. Neal relaxed slowly. He couldn't quite convince himself that it was all over. One instant, he knew, the man opposite him was ready to draw his gun and fire. And now he was placidly lighting a cigarette with fingers that were as steady as rocks.

The girl had been talking to the shopkeeper, showing him a withered paper in her hand, and now he turned to Neal, smiling nervously.

He pointed to the knife which Neal still held in his hand.

"Give to Missy," he said imploringly. "Belong her."

Neal hesitated an instant, and he was aware that the burning eyes of the girl's companion were resting unwaveringly on him.

"Please," the girl said simply.

Neal shrugged and handed the girl the knife. As his fingers met hers, he felt paper crackle under his fingers, felt a closely wadded note pushed against his palm. His fingers closed on it automatically and he shoved his fist in his pocket.

"Thank you," the girl said quickly.

She dropped the brilliantly gleaming knife into her handbag, turned, and left the shop. The thin, arrogant, steel-eyed man followed her without a backward glance.

"Go," the fat shopkeeper said nervously. "Go, please."

Neal pulled out the wad of paper and spread it flat against his hand. The only information it contained was the name of a hotel and a room number. Neal frowned and shoved it back into his pocket. That didn't tell him much about the screwy business.

He sauntered from the shop, his thoughts churning futilely. Quiet deliberation was not his most successful accomplishment and he felt queerly impotent and helpless. There was only one thing to do, he decided, after a few moments of anxious cogitation. He pulled the paper that the girl had slipped to him from his pocket and noted the address and room number. Then he walked on whistling.

THE soft Egyptian night had dropped its black mantle over Cairo, lending an almost mystic enchantment to the intertwined streets and the murmuring voices of natives. Under the merciful light of a full pale moon, the desert stretches surrounding the silent city, looked cool and calm and inviting. But those who knew the desert were aware of its ruthless reality, its cruelty, its danger.

The lobby of the Hotel International was practically deserted when Neal Kirby strolled across its polished floor and stopped at the desk of the blandly polite young native who acted as clerk and receptionist.

"Is the young lady in 402 in?" he asked.

The clerk nodded.

"Did you have an—"

"She's expecting me," Neal said quickly. Turning, he strode to the elevator. He realized disgustedly that he had acted tactlessly. The girl had taken such precautions in slipping him the note that it was obvious she didn't want it known that he was to see her. He had spoiled that by inquiring for her like a breathless sophomore.

He stepped from the elevator at the fourth floor. The hotel was completely modern, with luxuriously thick carpeting and walls paneled with smooth, dark oak. The heavy rug smothered the sounds of his footsteps as he started down the corridor, looking for 402.

He passed three doors before he found it. Suddenly he began to feel nervous. He paused before the door, his throat strangely dry. Maybe this whole thing was a joke of some sort. Or maybe he had received the note by mistake. A dozen other disturbing thoughts occurred to him, but he dismissed them all with a characteristic shrug. He raised his hand to knock when he heard a sudden scuffling noise from inside the room. It was followed by a quick, gasping cry of terror.

Neal hesitated for only a bare instant and then he grabbed the doorknob, shook it violently.

The door was locked. Neal drew back and lunged at the door, driving his heavy shoulders against its hard surface. A splintering crack sounded and the door swung inward suddenly, almost throwing him off balance.

The room was dark, but there was enough moonlight to show him the shadowy outline of two figures struggling near the window. In spite of the uncertain illumination he recognized one of the figures as the girl he had met in the curio shop. She was struggling helplessly against a man whose both hands were wrapped about her neck.

THE man looked up as Neal charged into the room. He dropped the limp body of the girl and sprang toward the window, which opened on the fire escape.

Neal dove across the room and his shoulder drove into the man's back, slamming him against the wall. He heard a grunt of pain escape the man's lips, but like an eel, the dark figure squirmed from his grasp and dove for the window.

Neal lunged after him, his right fist swinging in a wild looping arc. It crashed into the side of the man's head as he scrambled over the window ledge, knocking him out onto the balcony formed by the fire escape.

Neal threw the window open wider, but before he could clamber out his intended victim scrambled to his feet and darted down the steps. Neal had one quick look at the man's dark terrified features before he disappeared.

Wheeling from the window, Neal stepped quickly across the room and closed the door that he had forced. He groped about until he found a lamp and switched it on. He knew there would be no chance of catching the native who had fled down the fire escape, and the girl might be seriously hurt. She was lying on the floor next to a sofa, unconscious. There were angry red marks on her throat, but he could see the rise and fall of her breast under the light flimsy dressing gown she was wearing

He lifted her carefully in his arms, stretched her on the sofa, and rubbed her hands anxiously. After a moment or so her eyelids flickered and he noticed a touch of color returning to her cheeks. With her long, fine hair framing her white face she looked more like an angel than a human being.

She was breathing more normally now, Neal noticed. He poured a glass of water from a pitcher on the coffee table, tilted her head slightly, and poured some of its contents down her throat.

She coughed weakly and opened her eyes. For an instant she stared blankly at him, and then, as recognition came to her, she smiled tremulously.

"I was afraid you wouldn't come," she murmured. Her hands moved slowly to her throat, touched the abrasions on her skin.

"Don't talk if it hurts," Neal said, concerned. "What you need is rest."

"It doesn't hurt," the girl assured him. "I'm still a little frightened, that's all. Silly of me. I should be getting used to it by now."

"You mean this has happened before?" Neal asked incredulously.

The girl was silent an instant, and then she turned her eyes full on Neal. In them was mirrored the tragic finality of despair.

"I was wrong to involve you in my troubles," she said brokenly. "Please go now while there is still time. I—it may be dangerous for you to stay another minute."

Neal grinned cheerfully and tossed his hat onto an empty chair. He lighted a cigarette and blew a cloud of smoke toward the ceiling expansively.

"You can't get rid of me that easily," he chuckled.

"Oh please," the girl said miserably. "You think it's something of a lark, something amusing. Can't you see I'm serious?"

Neal's face sobered.

"The cute little chap who was trying to strangle you was serious too," he said drily. "That's why I'm sticking around until I know what's up. Funny streak in me. I dislike seeing young girls murdered. I don't know why. But everybody has their peculiarities and that happens to be mine."

"Would you like me to start at the beginning?" she asked abruptly.

"Now you're talking," Neal grinned. "I may not be of any help, but I'm in your corner from now on."

The girl relaxed as if a heavy weight had been removed from her shoulders.

"Thank you," she said simply. She was silent for a few seconds before resuming.

"MY name is Jane Manners," she said quietly. "My father was a well known archaeologist. When he died several years ago he left me a manuscript which contained a map and directions for reaching a city somewhere in the Egyptian desert. He had visited the city years before and it had been his consuming ambition to return there before he died. His last wish was that I would go there and complete the archaeological work he had begun. I didn't have the necessary funds so I put the trip off. Then I received an offer of help. It came from an Austrian, Max Zaraf, who said that he had known my father in Egypt."

"Was he the gent I met today?" Neal interrupted.

"Yes. He financed the expedition. At first I was delighted by the assistance, but things have happened which make me believe I made a very serious mistake."

"What sort of things?" Neal asked.

"In the first place," Jane answered, "he insisted that I let him keep the map. I gave it to him without hesitation. That same night I was almost killed by a heavy piece of iron that dropped from the deck above me. The officers on the boat were unable to explain the accident. Again, three nights later, I was almost killed by a knife hurled through my porthole. It missed me by inches."

Neal whistled silently.

"Why didn't you ask Zaraf to return the map to you and call the whole deal off?"

Jane shook her head miserably.

"I wasn't sure he had anything to do with it. I'm not yet, for that matter. And if I back out I may never get another opportunity to carry out Dad's last wishes."

Neal glanced down at his knuckles.

"Did it occur to you that it was too late to back out? That is, if Zaraf is the little dark boy in the woodpile. If he made two attempts on your life he certainly wouldn't give you back the map now and let you walk out on him at this late date. If you tried you'd just be sealing your own death warrant."

"I thought of that," Jane answered. "There wasn't anything to do but go along with him and hope for the best."

"Which won't be any too good, if I'm any judge of character," Neal said drily. "But what about the knife you got at the curio shop? How does that fit into the picture?"

"I don't know," Jane answered, frowning. "In Dad's manuscript he made it very clear that before starting the trip I should stop here in Cairo and pick up that knife. He left it here on his last trip. It must be important or he wouldn't have been so insistent about it. The shopkeeper knew him and had promised to keep the knife until he returned for it, or sent for it.

The paper which I showed the shopkeeper was written by Dad and was a sort of a claim-check on the knife."

"One more question," Neal grinned. "How did you happen to pick me for a Boy Scout?"

The girl smiled slightly.

"Maybe," she answered, "because you look like a Boy Scout. I scribbled my address on a piece of paper while you and Max were glaring at each other in the curio shop. Afterward I told myself that I had acted foolishly, that you'd never bother to investigate a silly, impulsive gesture like that."

"That was a serious mistake in judgment," Neal told her lightly.

As he finished speaking a hinge creaked faintly behind him. Then a suave icy voice said:

"A very serious mistake, indeed!"

NEAL didn't turn. Instead he watched Jane Manners. Her eyes looking over his shoulders were filled with a sudden, shocked fear.

"*Max!*" she whispered.

Neal stood up and turned slowly. Unconsciously his big hands tightened into hard, blocky fists. In the doorway, smiling without humor, stood Max Zaraf. The trailing smoke from the cigarette in his hand curled up past his lean, saturnine face, dimming slightly the cold, deadly glitter of his eyes. But Neal, watching the man closely, was sure there was disappointment in those eyes. Disappointment and a slight trace of uncertainty.

"Are you all right, my dear?" Zaraf asked softly, ignoring Neal.

Neal grinned, a tight mirthless grin. Zaraf acted as if he hadn't been expecting to find things quite as they were.

"Why shouldn't she be?" Neal asked, before Jane could answer.

Zaraf shrugged and stepped into the room. His eyes flicked menacingly to the shattered lock of the door.

"Logical question, isn't it?" he asked silkily. "Door forced open. Room upset. A tempestuous young American violating the privacy of a young woman's room. It all adds up, does it not?"

"Max!" Jane said sharply. "You're being insulting."

"You're also being very careless of your health," Neal said pointedly.

Zaraf turned slightly and looked straight at Neal. The slight smile vanished from his features. Neal saw a new, wary look creep into Zaraf's cold eyes, and he realized that the man had just recognized him as the American he had encountered at the curio shop.

"What is your game, my young friend?" he asked coolly. "This couldn't possibly be a coincidence. If it is, let me assure you that it might be a most unlucky one—for you."

"It is not a coincidence," Jane said quietly. "I asked Mister—" she faltered, and Neal realized that he hadn't told her his name.

"Kirby," he said quickly. "Neal Kirby. You must have forgot."

"Thank you," Jane said gratefully. "I asked Mr. Kirby to come here," she resumed, "because I thought I might need him."

"For what?" Zaraf asked.

Neal wondered what reason the girl would give for asking him here. To tell the truth would reveal to Zaraf her suspicions concerning him. He looked at her, and her eyes met his in an imploring glance, before she faced Zaraf. Her slender body stiffened and her chin raised slightly as she said:

"I have hired Mr. Kirby," she said clearly, "as consulting archaeologist. He will leave with us tomorrow morning."

ZARAF'S steely calm was shaken. "Are you out of your mind?" he asked hoarsely.

Neal stared at Jane in amazement. It was preposterous, out of the question, completely unthinkable. He didn't know a thing about archaeology in the first place, and secondly, why should he be wandering over the desert looking for lost cities? It didn't make sense.

Then he looked at Jane, and suddenly it did make sense. For some crazy reason it became the most logical thing in the world for him to go anywhere, do anything this girl wanted. She was looking at him beseechingly, hope and confidence shining in her eyes.

He turned to Zaraf, smiling faintly at the man's obvious consternation.

"That's right," he said cheerfully. "I'm the new archaeologist. I'm not such a hot archaeologist, but

I'm a pretty good shot and I hear the desert is just full of snakes and rats."

Zaraf struggled to restrain his anger. His cheeks were touched with red and his cold eyes were twin pools of hate. But his voice was as soft as silk as he said:

"You have to shoot a *snake* before it stings you. Remember that my young friend." He turned then, and with a mocking bow to the girl, left the room.

"Lovely fellow," Neal murmured.

"He's dangerous and cruel," Jane said worriedly. "I—I shouldn't have gotten you into this. I have a terrible feeling that I'll hate myself for it. If anything should happen to you, I'd feel as if it were my fault."

Neal picked up his hat and smiled down at her.

"Forget it," he said. He sauntered to the door, and grinned back at her. "I wasn't kidding, you know, when I told our chum that I was a pretty good shot. The fact is I'm a damn good shot. See you tomorrow."

THE tiny caravan of four camels and three attendants wound its way from Cairo the following day, as the blazing morning sun served notice that the day would be scorching hot.

Each camel carried a passenger, and was led by a native attendant at the end of a stout rope. The fourth camel carried huge leather sacks of water. It was roped to the last camel in the train and clumped awkwardly along, apparently unimpressed by the fact that it carried the most precious commodity of the desert—water.

On the lead camel rode Max Zaraf. Behind him rode Jane Manners and bringing up the rear was Neal Kirby, swaying awkwardly on his lurching steed, and feeling uncomfortable and strange in his pith helmet and breeches and boots.

Zaraf had the map in his possession and gave the directions of travel to the native guides. For two days the trip was monotonously uneventful, varying little in detail from hour to hour. They traveled for the most part in the cool of the morning and evening and laid up during the blistering heat of the day. The terrain was endlessly unchanging. Slight rises of sand gave way to sloping valleys that led only to still another hill.

On the evening of the third day Zaraf waved them to a stop and Neal climbed stiffly from his camel, glad to ease his muscles after a hard four-hour stretch. He walked through the soft sifting sand and assisted Jane Manners to alight. Zaraf was walking back toward them from his camel. They had stopped just below the summit of a rather high hill, and the fine top sand was blowing down on them in swirling, uncomfortable clouds.

"We stop here," Zaraf announced, coming up to them.

"Here?" Neal echoed. "Let's go over the hill to the valley. We'll get out of this wind that way."

The native drivers, dark-skinned and inscrutable, waited stolidly for orders. They were a proud, silent breed of men, neither volunteering information, nor expecting it. As long as they received their money for the day's work, it didn't matter what their white-skinned masters did.

Zaraf glared balefully at Neal.

"I have said we will stop here," he repeated angrily. "I'm deciding on our course and if I decide to stop here it's because I have excellent reasons for doing so."

Neal shrugged. It seemed a small matter to argue about. Maybe Zaraf did have a good reason for stopping here.

"Okay," he said, "if you can stand the sand I guess Jane and I can put up with it."

Zaraf turned without a word and walked back to his camel. The natives went to work building a shelter, and preparing the evening meal. The camels, relieved of their packs, settled placidly down on their haunches, like so many quiet cows.

Darkness fell swiftly. Neal said goodnight to Jane and turned in early. The fires burned out in a few hours and before the moon came up the tiny camp was slumbering.

NEAL awoke the following morning as the first rays of the rising sun slanted into his eyes. He blinked sleepily and yawned. His first thought was of water. Every morning he awoke thirsty, for the desert's searing heat dried out the moisture in his body as he slept. He climbed to his feet, stuck his feet into his boots, and pulled on his shirt. Then he crawled out of the narrow pup tent, straightened up and looked around.

For an instant he stared about unbelievingly. The camels and the native guides were nowhere in sight. The black ashes of the evening's fire still showed as cancerous spots against the whiteness of the sand, but the natives sleeping gear and packs—and more vital, the camels—were vanished as completely as if the earth had opened and swallowed them.

For seconds Neal was too stupefied to act. All he could do was stare in numbed bewilderment at the bleak expanse of the desert.

When his dazed senses finally recovered, he wheeled and charged toward the other two sleeping tents.

"Zaraf! Jane!" he shouted. "On your feet. Our guides have pulled a fade-out with the equipment and camels."

He was so excited that he did not notice the abysmal silence that seemed to stretch over the desert like a vast tight blanket.

Reaching Zaraf's tent he jerked open the flap. He opened his mouth but the excited words on his lips died there. For Zaraf's sleeping pad was undisturbed. It had obviously not been used that night.

Neal felt the cold of panic close over his heart. For a silent, timeless instant he stared incredulously at Zaraf's empty tent—then he was racing madly through the thick sand toward Jane's tent. He shouted her name wildly and the hills threw back the mockery of an echo.

"People of the Pyramids" originally appeared in the December, 1941 issue of *Fantastic Adventures* magazine; cover shown above

He ripped open the flap without waiting for an answer to his shout. One glance showed him it was empty. The sleeping pad had been used, for it was twisted and tossed into a jumbled heap. Neal's eyes picked quickly about the interior, noticing the generally disarrayed condition of the sleeping articles and clothes. One corner of the tent sagged drunkenly inward, and he could see that the rope and peg had pulled out of place. Everything pointed to a struggle or roughhouse of some sort. Neal stood up, a frantic fear clawing at his attempted calmness. As far as his eye could reach, the desert sands spread in a never-varying, never-ending expanse of sun and heat.

"Jane!" he shouted desperately.

"Jane! ...Jane!"

The echo mocked him.

Neal peered into Jane's tent again. A comb and hairbrush were lying on the canvas floor, along with her wristwatch and a ring she usually wore. Neal's frown deepened. Jane wouldn't have left things like that if—if—

One inevitable conclusion forced itself on him. Zaraf had taken Jane by force, and with the camels and water, deserted in the dark of the night. There was no other conclusion possible. Neal realized then, with sickening abruptness, that in all probability this had been in Zaraf's mind from the outset.

NEAL rested on his haunches in Jane's tent and thought carefully for a few moments. He had no water, no food, and no means of transportation. His revolver had three shots left in it. The rest of the ammunition was in the camel packs. Except for the sun he had not the slightest means of gauging direction or ascertaining a definite course even if he had one to follow.

Approximately, he had thirty-six hours to live.

"Okay," he muttered to himself. The pleasantness had gone from his features; leaving his face a stiff, expressionless mask. "It's a slim chance, but I'll take it. I may not find you, Max Zaraf but God help you if I do!"

He was crawling from Jane's tent when his hand touched the rent in the canvas. It was an inch-long rip close to the flap opening.

Obeying a strange impulse, Neal examined it closely. He shoved his finger through the tear and wiggled it about in the warm sand beneath the flooring. Suddenly his finger touched something that was not sand. Something that was as cool and hard and smooth as—steel!

Quickly Neal ripped the canvas flooring aside and dug into the sand with both hands. A second later he drew from the sand a glittering object which he recognized instantly.

It was the bejeweled knife which he had accidentally stumbled on in the curio shop in Cairo. He recognized it instantly by the handle, formed as a human torso, and the human head which topped it. The flashing necklace of diamonds scintillated brilliantly in the dim light of the tent.

Neal laughed bitterly and shoved it into his pocket. It was worth a great amount of money, men had probably fought and died over it, but it couldn't buy him a drop of water now.

He retrieved his pith helmet from his own tent and started out. Plowing awkwardly through the burning sand, he headed for the top of the hill, that led, he knew with bitter irony, to just another hill. But still he had to keep on. There was something inside of him, as strong as life itself, which would drive him on until...

NEAL KIRBY had given himself thirty-six hours of life. Now, he realized vaguely, as he lurched forward, he was twelve hours past that limit already. Living on borrowed time so to speak. His face was matted with sand clogged beard and his red-rimmed eyes were like hot points of fire in the blackness of his face.

For two days he had staggered through the blinding heat of the desert without food, without water. He had passed the limits of human endurance, but still he lurched on, some inner voice lashing him forward when his flagging body would quit.

He fell often. Sometimes he lay stretched on the burning sands for minutes before he could crawl back to his feet and stagger on again.

It was almost noon, now, and the sun seemed to be hanging suspended in the sky about a hundred feet above his aching head. He could actually feel the weight of the heat settling on him like a dense, smothering pall. Overhead soaring vultures were converging on his stumbling figure in ever narrowing circles.

Staggering over the top of a hill Neal saw the first sight to relieve the deadly monotony of the desert. Just what it was he couldn't tell, but it looked like a bundle of rags thrown together in a pile at the foot of the slight rise. With a strange flickering hope burning in his breast, Neal made a pathetic effort to run. He fell and slid most of the way, but at the foot of the hill he regained his feet and staggered on. Suddenly from the cluttered dark bundles which he had seen there, arose a small cloud of birds, their hideously flapping wings carrying them away from this one other thing on the desert that lived beside themselves.

Neal stopped short, almost gagging. He was close enough to recognize the bundles now as three human forms. Numbly he approached them. Sprawled on the sand with bullet holes in their heads, were the three native guides who had accompanied Zaraf into the desert. Neal stared at them for seconds in dumb silence. Zaraf's treachery had not ended with deserting him in the desert. Here was mute testimony of that.

In spite of everything Neal felt a vicious satisfaction course through him. The bodies of the native guides were unmistakable signposts telling him that he was at least on the right track. The canteens of the native guides were empty so he staggered on again, somehow strengthened by the realization that he couldn't be many hours behind Jane and Zaraf.

An hour later he fell. He was on top of another hill overlooking a broad, sloping valley, identical to the other interminable valleys he had crossed, except that this one seemed longer and wider than most of the others. For a half-hour he lay on his stomach trying to find the will and the strength to go on. He heard a faint whir above and turned weakly just as a huge cadaverous vulture was settling on him. With a hoarse croak of fright the bird veered off and glided down into the valley. Neal hoisted himself painfully to his knees and drew his gun. Why he was so bent on killing the bird he couldn't have told himself. He rested the revolver on his forearm and sighted carefully. The bird was gliding into the valley soaring within six feet of the ground when Neal fired.

HE missed. The bird flapped great wings and climbed into the sky to resume his endless circling. But a strange reverberating echo had started across the valley. It magnified the report of the pistol a dozen times until it seemed as if mighty hammers were drumming maddeningly on the ground. Neal listened wonderingly.

Suddenly he noticed a peculiar distortion of the heat waves that were dancing in front of his eyes. Their gossamer lightness and fantastically odd shapes were dissolving and resorting themselves before his eyes. It was as if all the light waves and heat waves of the valley were broken to bits by the crescendoing clamor of the echoes which were booming across the valley.

The entire atmosphere of the valley, he noticed, was vibrating visibly. Crazy lances of light shot into the sky and the distorted refractions of sun and heat waves merged together into what looked like solid blocks of light. In the center of the valley there appeared a shining shaft of pure white light that was growing wider by the second.

Neal climbed shakily to his feet, stunned.

The shaft continued to widen and he saw then that it was not composed of light, but some material that looked like white marble.

The thunderous drumming of the echo culminated in one great crash that seemed mighty enough to shatter the heavens. Then silence settled oppressively over the valley.

The white shaft of marble was widening swiftly now, as if some vast invisible curtain was being drawn back in front of it. Neal watched in fascination as a mighty structure of marble appeared before his eyes, filling the entire valley, and almost piercing the clouds with its majestic peak of glittering white. It was formed in the shape of a pyramid, alabaster white, incredibly huge.

The silence was complete now and the fantastic distortions of the atmosphere had ceased. The valley was quiet and tranquil as when he first saw it. Everything was the same except for the appearance of the magnificent white pyramid towering into the heavens.

Neal sagged to his knees. If it was a mirage, it was the most impressive and authentic he'd ever heard of. He was still looking at the gigantic pyramid when he saw the orange bolt of flame flash from its base. It seemed a whip of flame with a large ball of some brightly burning matter attached to it. When he saw that it was heading for him he tried to run, as a man runs from the unknown, but it was too late. Something caressed the back of his head like a hot breath and he stumbled onto his face. The next instant a smothering blanket of blackness settled over him and everything faded out abruptly.

WHEN Neal came to he was lying on a narrow cot in a small room. There were no windows that he could see, only one small opening that might be a door. He struggled to a sitting position on the cot. The first thing he realized was that he wasn't thirsty. His lips were still cracked and tender, but he knew from their feel that water had passed over them. His hand touched his matted three-day beard experimentally, and his eyes traveled in mild disgust over his dirty, ragged breeches and scuffed boots.

He leaned back and wondered where he was. Thinking accurately was a difficult proposition. His conscious memory was that of a fantastic white pyramid which had materialized before him on the desert. Before that he had been close on the trail of Max Zaraf and Jane Manners. That thought jolted him.

He climbed to his feet and looked around. The walls were of a peculiar porous material and they seemed to be the source of the pale, glareless illumination that flooded the tiny room. There was no furniture other than the narrow cot, and the small door was locked in some manner from the outside. The problem of getting out, he decided, was not going to be easy.

He sank back onto the cot despairingly. All he could do was wait. An hour passed before he heard a clicking on the outside of the door. Then it swung inward. Neal saw a highly polished boot, white whipcord breeches, and then the tall, gaunt figure of Max Zaraf filled the narrow doorway. His freshly shaven features were touched with a mocking smile and his cold eyes gleamed with sardonic amusement.

"This is a pleasure I hadn't counted on," he said, smiling.

For a stunned instant Neal was too dazed to speak. Even in his astonishment, however, one thing was obvious. Zaraf was in the saddle now or he wouldn't be so completely cool and nonchalant. Every instinct in his body urged him to hurl himself at Zaraf's relaxed figure and throttle the life from the man, but a bump of common sense warned him to proceed cautiously and wait for an opportunity.

"I don't imagine you had counted on seeing me again," he said as easily as he could. "Most men stranded in the desert die there."

"But you didn't," Zaraf smiled. "How persistent of you."

"I had something to live for," Neal answered quietly.

Zaraf shrugged.

"The past is dead," he said, still smiling. "Since you lived through the desert I might give you the chance to continue living. However, that is up to you. If you are willing to do as I say, it can be arranged. If not," he spread his hands in an expressive gesture, "your gallant fight through the desert will be of no avail."

"It is my great pleasure," Neal said recklessly, "to tell you to go to hell. If I had nine lives I'd sacrifice'em all before I'd lower myself to bargain with a treacherous, rotten snake like you."

Zaraf continued to smile, but two hot flags of color fluttered in his cheeks.

"I came here to offer you a chance for your life. You could have helped me here but that is not to be. For your information we are approximately five hundred feet underground right now. We are in the lost city which Professor Manners discovered. It was never actually a lost city, but rather a hidden city. A strange race of people have developed here, many of them childishly simple in many ways. It is to be my privilege to teach them the benefits of commercialization. You might have helped me and done very well for yourself. It was only an accident that you discovered the secret of the pyramid, but it is an accident which might have been profitable to you." He smiled blandly down at Neal. "Many of the charmingly simple people love pageantry and drama so I'll have to devise a spectacular manner in which to usher you into the Great Beyond."

"Where is Jane?" Neal asked suddenly.

"Ahh," Zaraf smiled. "That worries you, does it? Well Jane is not too happy, but I have strong hopes that under my persuasive technique I can make her learn to enjoy the existence I've planned for her."

As he finished speaking he bowed slightly and stepped through the door. It closed immediately behind him.

NEAL paced the narrow room nervously for the next hour. The realization that Jane was near him, possibly within a few hundred feet of him, was maddening. Maddening too, was the realization that she was in Zaraf's hands, helpless. Another hour, as nearly as he could judge, had passed when he heard the faint click of the lock. He paused and watched the door carefully. It swung inward, an inch at a time, until it stood open.

Neal doubled his fists and spread his legs. If a chance to smash his way out of this cell presented itself he was going to grab it.

Seconds later a young girl stepped cautiously into the room. Her skin was a pallid white in color and her large eyes were twin mirrors of fright. She was small and her thin body was trembling under the loose white garment she wore. Her hair was long, and would have been considered beautiful, were it not so dull and lusterless.

Neal unclenched his fists slowly. He had been prepared for just about anything, but this peculiar looking, frightened girl stopped him completely. Her eyes were on his now, and she seemed trying desperately to make him understand something.

Finally she held her fingers over her mouth and Neal gathered that she wanted him to keep silent.

Then she reached out and took his hand in her own and pointed through the doorway with her other hand. Her meaning was clear enough to Neal. She wanted him to follow her, but why? Neal didn't stop to argue the question with himself. It might be a trap, but it wasn't likely that they would go to such elaborate lengths to lure him from the cell. Anyway it was better than doing nothing. He decided to follow the girl.

"Lead on, sister," he whispered. "If you're on the level, God bless you."

The girl led him into the corridor that flanked the room in which he had been confined. Looking about he could tell nothing about where he was or where he was going. The walls were blue, and of the same porous composition that constituted the walls of the room he had just left. The corridor stretched ahead endlessly and Neal noticed that every six feet or so a door was built into the wall, identical with the one that led to the room which he had just left. The ceiling was high and vaulted, but was without ornamentation of any sort.

The girl crept softly ahead of him, glancing frequently back to see that he was still following. In another hundred feet they turned at right angles and followed another corridor. For fifteen or twenty minutes they continued, twisting and turning through the labyrinthine passages that interlaced each other at odd angles. Finally the girl stopped at a door, that seemed to Neal identical to the hundreds of others they had passed, and pressed her ear against its surface.

After a silent interval she opened the door cautiously and motioned for Neal to go in. Neal hesitated an instant. If there was anything phony about the set-up this was where the payoff would be. With a mental shrug he stepped over the threshold and into the room.

"Neal, darling!" a wonderfully familiar voice cried.

"JANE!" Neal whispered unbelievingly. For an instant he stood rooted to the spot, too amazed to move. This had been the farthest thing from his thoughts. She was standing at the opposite side of the room, and in her eyes was relief and joy that made his heart pound faster. She was wearing a loose flowing gown of white and it gave her blonde beauty an almost ethereal quality.

Recovering he crossed to her, took her hands in his.

"Honey," he said fervently, "you're the most welcome sight I've seen in all my life. Are you all right? Has that swine done anything to you?"

"I'm all right," she said breathlessly.

"I heard that you had been brought here and the little girl who is my attendant was willing to take a message to you. Finally she thought she could bring you here easier. She's watching in the hall now so we have a few minutes to talk."

"What's this all about?" Neal asked. "Where are we?"

"We're in the city my father discovered," she answered. "It's underground. A whole tribe of people—offshoots of some highly cultivated desert group—built it as a retreat against their more savage neighbors centuries ago. Here they have progressed amazingly well along certain lines, in electricity for instance, but in other fields they are childishly ignorant."

"Zaraf knew my father years ago and knew that he made this discovery. So his offer to help me was because he wanted access to this city for purposes of exploitation. We arrived here just a few days ahead of you, but fortunately for Zaraf, an evil element of the natives has been planning a revolution against the established ruling system. Being an opportunist Zaraf jumped right in with the revolvers and helped them overthrow their ruler."

"And that makes him ace-high with the new management," Neal said reflectively.

Jane nodded.

"He told me all his plans the day after he kidnapped me and left you stranded in the desert. He was sure you were out of the picture forever. He intends to work himself into a position of power, regiment these natives, sell their produce and electrical equipment to the highest bidders. He must be stopped, Neal, he must. These natives are, for the most part, simple and kindly, but they're easily influenced by white people because they worshipped my father. He was very kind and good to them during the years he stayed here, and Zaraf is trading on that."

"Our big job," Neal said, "is to get out of here as fast as we can. Do you have any idea of the size of this place? Or where we are now in relation to the nearest exit?"

Jane shook her head.

"I'm completely lost," she confessed. "I know, however, that we are in one of the larger sleeping sections now. Everyone is up at the throne hall at this time to hear the new instructions from the new ruler. His name is Horjak. That's why it was safe to bring you here through the halls. All the rooms are deserted now. Most of the natives here aren't sympathetic with the new regime, but they are helpless because they have no leader or weapons."

Neal started to speak but a shrill terrified shriek from beyond the door interrupted him. It was followed instantly by a loud banging on the panels. Neal heard a harsh voice snapping commands and he knew that Zaraf was outside.

JANE was clinging to his arm desperately.

"You've got to get out of here, darling," she cried.

This was the grim truth, Neal admitted, but there was no other exit from the room. He disengaged Jane's frantic grip on his arm and shoved her into a corner, just as the door crashed inward.

Three small, but heavily muscled men, with the same pallid expression and lusterless hair of the young native girl, spilled into the room. They wore crimson tunics that dropped to the middle of their thighs and sandals with soft spongy soles. They sprang at Neal with a concerted ferocity that amazed him. The first soldier went down under a sledgehammer right hook that carried all of Neal's heavy shoulder behind it. But before he could swing again the other two grabbed his arms. More of the crimson-tunicked guards poured into the room and the struggle was over. Panting, he was dragged from the room into the corridor to face the coldly sneering presence of Max Zaraf.

"I gave you your chance," Zaraf snapped. "You refused it. Now you can accept your alternate choice." He motioned imperiously to the guards. "To the throne room. Quickly!" Before the guards could move to obey his order Jane rushed into the corridor and blocked their path with outstretched hands.

"You can't do this," she cried to Zaraf. "I won't let you."

Zaraf smiled at her, cynically.

"Since you are so perturbed as to his fate," he said silkily, "I think it would be interesting if you would witness the execution yourself. There's nothing like the presence of a lovely woman to inspire a man to die a hero's death." He nodded to two of the guards. "Take her along."

The husky, crimson-tunicked guards sprang to obey, and after a brief, unequal struggle, the girl was carried away after Neal.

THE throne room was a vast hall lined with tier upon tier of seats extending up to the highest reaches of the amphitheater. In the center of the throne room a huge unadorned dais was erected and on it sprawled a corpulent figure with an overly large head and dense stupid features.

Neal saw all this in one quick glance as he was shoved through a lower tier aisle and led to the large oval enclosure that faced the throne. The entire hall was brilliantly illuminated by the same sort of indirect lighting he had noticed before. Standing next to the figure on the throne was Max Zaraf, a gloating smile of anticipation on his face.

The throne room was quiet, but the tiers of seats were jammed with the native population of the underground city. Neal noticed the silence particularly. It was the brooding silence of a death block before an execution.

Zaraf bowed slightly to the figure on the dais and stepped down to face Neal.

"Very shortly," he said, "you are going to die in a quite spectacular manner. You are a fool and you deserve it. These people are incredibly brilliant in many things, many things which the outside world will pay steeply for. Their invisibility screen with which they surround their central pyramid is one instance. Your pistol shot accidentally disrupted the force field and thus you accidentally stumbled onto the pyramid."

"The blue death, which they can send for fifty feet or fifty miles, is one of the most destructive weapons the world will ever know. In your case they used a light charge which knocked you out, but they can use it to wipe out whole cities."

"Things like that are more valuable than diamonds in the world today. With clever exploitation who knows how far I can go?" Zaraf smiled and there was a sinister ugliness in the effort. "You, however, Mr. Meddler are not going any farther at all. At my demand Horjak, the new ruler, has ordered your execution. It will be followed by wholesale executions of those who oppose the reign of Horjak."

"A very nice setup," Neal said quietly. "Those you don't approve of, or who don't approve of you, just get wiped out. It may work, Zaraf, but you'll find living with yourself quite a job."

"I can stand it, I think," Zaraf chuckled mirthlessly. "Now to get down to business. My real reason in coming down here was to point out the highly ingenious method I have selected for your elimination."

He pointed to a rack-like affair that was raised from the floor six or seven feet.

"In words of one syllable," Zaraf continued with relish, "you will be spread-eagled there, tied hand and foot to each of the four posts. Then at a signal from me, the executioner cuts a very slender cord and the most amazing thing happens."

He pointed up to the right and left of the rack, and Neal saw for the first time that half dozen huge knives were suspended by ropes from the ceiling, parallel to the rack.

"The knives swing down," Zaraf said softly. "They are heavy and will travel very fast. They will pass through your suspended body and that will be that! Your wrists and ankles will still be attached to the posts but the rest of your body will be sliced as neatly as a sausage. Clever, isn't it?"

IN SPITE of himself, Neal felt a horrible revulsion crawling over him. To die was one thing. But to die like a butchered hog in front of a howling mob of savages was quite another.

His eyes circled the arena desperately. Every exit was guarded with a dozen men, every aisle clogged with spectators. His gaze swung back to Zaraf and he used every ounce of will power in his control to force a smile over his features.

"Am I supposed to be frightened?" he asked softly. "Am I supposed to be trembling and begging for mercy now? Sorry to disappoint you, Zaraf, but it doesn't worry me that much."

Zaraf's face flushed an angry red, but without another word, he turned and marched up the steps to the dais. Neal's eyes followed him and then he saw Jane.

Pale and regal, she was standing next to the dais, her arms bound behind her. Neal felt a cold sweat break out on his body. They *couldn't* let her watch. It wasn't human.

Zaraf turned and smiled down at Neal.

"Remember to be your most heroic," he said mockingly. "We have distinguished company present."

The crimson-tunicked guards stepped forward now and grabbed Neal by the arms. His eyes were on Jane, and he hardly felt them shoving him toward the rack.

He was trying desperately, frantically to tell her with his eyes that he loved her and would always love her, wherever he might be. He had never said the things he wanted to say to her and this was his last opportunity.

Suddenly a clear, terrible scream of anguish sounded through the vast, packed throne room.

"You can't! You can't! Let me die with him!" It was Jane sobbing and crying frantically, stumbling down the steps of the dais toward the execution rack.

"You fool!" shouted Zaraf. "Come back here!"

Leaping from his chair he plunged down the steps after her. Shouts and yells sounded through the throne room, as the natives lent their voices to the excitement.

Neal turned at Jane's scream. The two guards holding him relaxed their grip in the general confusion. With a sudden writhing twist Neal was free. He was weakened from his exposure in the desert, but his right hook was still a dangerous weapon. His first swing caught the guard off balance and dumped him in a complete somersault to the ground. Two more guards rushed at him, but he sidestepped them with a quick leap. As he landed he felt something jab into his thigh with an agonizing pain. Instinctively his hand moved to the spot, his fingers touched a slim, hard object close to his thigh. A surge of hope shot through him, not that he could hope to win, but that at least he could put up an excellent account for himself.

The two guards were closing in on him now, but before they could grab him, his hand flashed from his pocket grasping the strange, diamond-studded knife that he had first seen in the Cairo curio shop and secondly, when he had found it under the canvas flooring of Jane's tent. He had shoved it into his pocket then and forgotten it. His hand closed about the torso-handle of the knife now, and the diamond necklace that topped the torso flashed in a thousand scintillating sparkles as he drew his arm back to slash out at the two guards who were pressing him.

But his arm did not fall! It remained rigidly aloft as though frozen.

FOR the two guards were staring at the knife, fearfully tremblingly. Hoarse, guttural pleas sounded inarticulately from their throats as they backed away from him, terror-stricken. When they were eight feet from him they suddenly hurled themselves to the floor and groveled there, mouthing strange incantations. Neal wheeled, and as he flashed the knife about his head, the other guards dropped to their knees, their voices blending with the first two guards.

Taking advantage of this sudden, but inexplicable break, Neal leaped toward the base of the dais where Jane was struggling helplessly with Zaraf. Horjak, the new ruler, saw Neal charge toward the dais brandishing the scintillating knife in his hand like an avenging angel. With a soft moan of terror he sank to his knees, babbling incoherently.

Zaraf flung Jane to one side and leaped past Neal. He sprinted to the oval enclosure where the guards were moaning and groveling on their faces.

"Get up!" he screamed. "Get up you yellow hounds. Grab the prisoner and tear him apart with your hands. Get up! Get up!"

But he might have been talking to lumps of clay or sodden logs for all the attention the guards paid his hysterical commands. There was a swelling moaning noise coming now from the rows of packed seats. On their knees and on their faces the natives moaned and chanted their mysterious mumbling incantations.

Neal clasped Jane to him and slashed her bonds with the glittering knife, and then he jumped from the dais and started after Zaraf.

Zaraf saw him coming. With one last frantic scream at the oblivious natives, he turned blindly and dashed under the rack. His foot caught on a silken cord and hurled him to the ground, but he clambered quickly to his feet.

Then he screamed—madly and hysterically, once.

Neal saw it happen, saw the complete, incredibly horrible death by which Max Zaraf paid for his sins.

His foot had tripped the knife release under the rack, and when he sprang to his feet, the heavy, speeding knives—poised for Neal's execution—flashed downward with the devastating force of razor-sharp cleavers. Twelve blades there were, and each one found at least part of its target.

SHAKEN, Neal made his way to Jane's side. She was slumped at the foot of the dais, sobbing. He slipped his arm around her shoulder.

"It's all over darling," he murmured softly. "I think we can straighten things out now."

He looked up as a calm, wise looking old man with long white hair approached slowly.

"I am a friend," the old man said softly. "I am not afraid of the knife of Sali, the Goddess of Death. For I gave it to Professor Manners when he was here so many years ago. It was a pledge of our friendship and he always promised that he would bring it with him on his return."

"Why are the people afraid of it?" Neal asked.

The old man shrugged.

"People are afraid of things they do not understand. Years, centuries ago, it was believed by my people that Death was a woman who chose her victims in the dark and killed them with just such a knife as you hold in your hand. That knife was venerated by our people and prayed to, that it might spare them its sting. It was believed invincible."

"As ruler, I discouraged such outmoded beliefs, and to further eliminate the belief I gave the sacred knife of Sali to Professor Manners. But I have been deposed as ruler, and under the influences of barbaric customs once again, you see how quickly, my children revert to the beliefs and customs of their fathers."

"A lucky thing for us they did," Neal said. "What goes now? Will you take your job back as ruler around here?"

The white haired old man smiled.

"If my people want me," he said simply, "I will be happy to retain my authority."

Neal put his hand under Jane's chin and lifted her head up.

"No more crying now," he whispered.

"Everything's all set. The regular ruler is stepping back into the job and he's a great old guy. Why—why I'll bet he can even marry people!"

THE END

AUTHOR PORTRAIT

William P. McGivern (1918-1982)

If you've enjoyed this book, you will not want to miss these terrific titles…

ARMCHAIR LOST WORLD-LOST RACE CLASSICS, $12.95 each

B-48 **THE DRUMS OF TAPAJOS, Illustrated Edition**
by S. P. Meek

B-49 **THE TEMPLE OF FIRE, Illustrated Edition**
by Fred Ashley

B-50 **THE FACE IN THE ABYSS, and Other Fantastic Tales, Illust. Ed.**
by A. Merritt

B-51 **INLAND DEEP, Illustrated Edition**
by Richard Tooker

B-52 **THE SILVER GOD OF THE ORANG HUTAN, Illustrated Edition**
by David Douglas

B-53 **THE KING OF THE DEAD**
by Frank Aubrey

B-54 **THE BOATS OF THE GLEN CARRIG, Illustrated Edition**
by William Hope Hodgson

B-55 **THE SECRET OF THE EARTH**
by Charles Willing Beale

B-56 **THE WORLD OF THE GIANT ANTS, Illustrated Edition**
by A. Hyatt Verrill

B-57 **PHALANXES OF ATLANS, Illustrated Edition**
by F. Van Wyck Mason

ARMCHAIR CLASSICS OF SCIENCE FICTION SERIES, $12.95 each

C-80 **OPERATION: OUTER SPACE**
by Murray Leinster

C-81 **THE FIRE PEOPLE, Special Illustrated Edition**
by Ray Cummings

C-82 **THE BLACK STAR PASSES, Special Illustrated Edition**
by John W. Campbell

ARMCHAIR SCI-FI & HORROR GEMS SERIES, $12.95 each

G-29 **SCIENCE FICTION GEMS, Vol. Fifteen**
Milton Lesser and others

G-30 **HORROR GEMS, Vol. Fifteen**
Henry Kuttner and others

If you've enjoyed this book, you will not want to miss these terrific titles…

ARMCHAIR LOST WORLD-LOST RACE CLASSICS, $12.95 each

If you've enjoyed this book, you will not want to miss these terrific titles…

ARMCHAIR SCI-FI & HORROR DOUBLE NOVELS, $12.95 each

D-81   **THE LAST PLEA** by Robert Bloch
OMEGA by Robert Sheckley

D-82   **WOMAN FROM ANOTHER PLANET** by Frank Belknap Long
HOMECALLING by Judith Merril

D-83   **WHEN TWO WORLDS MEET** by Robert Moore Williams
THE MAN WHO HAD NO BRAINS by Jeff Sutton

D-84   **THE SPECTRE OF SUICIDE SWAMP** by E. K. Jarvis
IT'S MAGIC, YOU DOPE! by Jack Sharkey

D-85   **THE STARSHIP FROM SIRIUS** by Rog Phillips
THE FINAL WEAPON by Everett Cole

D-86   **TREASURE ON THUNDER MOON** by Edmond Hamilton
TRAIL OF THE ASTROGAR by Henry Hasse

D-87   **THE VENUS ENIGMA** by Joe Gibson
THE WOMAN IN SKIN 13 by Paul W. Fairman

D-88   **THE MAD ROBOT** by William P. McGivern
THE RUNNING MAN by J. Holly Hunter

D-89   **VENGEANCE OF KYVOR** by Randall Garrett
AT THE EARTH'S CORE by Edgar Rice Burroughs

D-90   **DWELLERS OF THE DEEP** by Don Wilcox
NIGHT OF THE LONG KNIVES by Fritz Leiber

ARMCHAIR SCIENCE FICTION CLASSICS, $12.95 each

C-28   **THE MAN FROM TOMORROW**
by Stanton A. Coblentz

C-29   **THE GREEN MAN OF GRAYPEC**
by Festus Pragnell

C-30   **THE SHAVER MYSTERY, Book Four**
by Richard S. Shaver

ARMCHAIR MASTERS OF SCIENCE FICTION SERIES, $16.95 each

MS-7   **MASTERS OF SCIENCE FICTION AND FANTASY, Vol. Seven**
Lester del Rey, "The Band Played On" and other tales

MS-8   **MASTERS OF SCIENCE FICTION, Vol. Eight**
Milton Lesser, "'A' is for Android" and other tales

Made in the USA
Middletown, DE
20 August 2023

37039768R00120